The Old Man is Dead

A Dirt Road Crime Story

Jason L. Queen

This is a work of fiction. Names, characters, organizations, places, events, and incidents are either products of the author's imagination or are used fictitiously. Any resemblance to actual persons, living or dead, or actual events is purely coincidental.

FIRST EDITION

Cover and layout design by Book Brewers

Marketing and Distribution by Independent Literature Brewing Company, Winchester, Virginia

For more information visit www.bookbrewers.com
or email jasonlqueen@bookbrewers.com

Printed in the United States of America

ISBN 978-1-7360070-6-8

The Old Man Is Dead

A Dirt Road Crime Story

This Book Is Dedicated To Everyone Who Has Had To Start Life Over Again Because You Totally Tanked Your First Try. Even Though There's No Reset Button For Life, There Is Always A Brand New Day. Until There Isn't.

Prologue

"I knew it. I told you I hooked something good!"

"Let's just wait and see, why don't we?"

"Wait and see what, dumbass?"

"What you actually caught, and who is actually the dumbass. Because I think you caught nothing. And I think it's you that's the–"

"That ain't no way to talk to your oldest son. I already know what it is."

"What the hell is it, then? And you're my only son, dumbass."

"It's a wheelchair."

"It's too dark to see. How can you tell?"

"I just know."

"Well, I'm wearing my headlamp and you left yours in the truck, so I can see better than you, and I can't tell what it is."

"Well shine it brighter and wait and see, Daddy. Wait. And. See."

"I'll wait and see alright. Damn, I love me some magnet fishin'. I told you it was better than the regular kind."

"It ain't better than catfishin'. Not even close."

"It's way better. Remember last week when I caught that big tool box. It was empty, but it could've been full. Imagine all those tools we could've caught. When's the last time you saw somebody catch a toolbox while catfishin'? I can answer my own question on your behalf. Never. To catch something like that requires intentionality."

"Well, maybe I was intentioning on catching this here wheelchair."

"I'm reserving my judgement until we take a closer look at it."

"Please do. I don't want you having no excuses and trying to take back your compliment, which I will wait for patiently. I just gotta land this sumbeech and drag it into the light here."

"Right. Right. Drag it on up next to the Bronco, boy. I'll switch on the headlights."

"I can't pull it in no more. It's sunk back down and stuck in the mud."

"Just ask for my help, baby boy. You know I don't mind. Stubborn little possum."

"I don't need your damn help. I get along just fine. I'm thirty years old. I don't need your help."

"It looks like you do. That rope ain't moved since that chair sunk back down. Is it caught on something?"

"It must be. Get your old ass on over here and help me, why dontcha? Why you waitin' over there in the dark like some kinda child snatcher?"

"Weak ass boy. Move back and let me get holt of it."

"Pull on it old man. That's right."

"You pull too, boy. Pull that rope like you're depending on what's on the other end of it to feed you tomorrow because you are. Nothin' to sell? Nothin' to eat."

"Let me grab back on it, too then. But just cause I'm pullin' don't mean you can stop pullin' you gray haired old bastard."

"I was just resting my elbows. Now let me show you how it's done. Yaahhhhhhhhhhh."

"Pull it on up under the Bronco lights. I told you it was a wheelchair."

"Damn son."

"Daddy, is that…?"

"It is. It damn sure is."

"It's a skeleton."

"Part of one, son. Part of one. Damn if that ain't the ribcage and his crotchetal bones."

"What the hell is crotchetal bones?"

"You know. The bones that make up his...crotch area. See there? He's got rope wrapped all around him, tying what's left of him to this here wheelchair."

"Does this mean we don't get to eat tomorrow, Daddy?"

Chapter 1

What had to be one of the last few phones still attached to an old fashioned landline rang until the equally antiquated answering machine picked up. A woman's voice said, "You've reached Buchanan Private Investigations. Leave your name and number and a very brief summary of your case." A man's voice in the background of the recording yelled, "If it isn't brief, the machine cuts you off, and if the machine cuts you off, I'm not calling you back." The woman's voice could be heard saying something, presumably to the man before she came back on after a quick moment and said, "Please leave a message after the beep. Thank you."

The machine then beeped and a young man spoke. "Yes. I'm calling to get some help. I was told that you help with cases like mine. I didn't know who else to call or ask. The police aren't helping. Nobody wants to help. Jonathan Baxter over at the bank told me you help with this kind of stuff. I sure hope you do. Mr. Baxter said you did. Anyways, uh… My name is Larry Robertson. My number is--" The machine beeped and cut off the man's voice.

The front door of the singlewide trailer opened, letting in light and dust before a tall man walked through the door. He fit the time period of the phone and the machine and the old trailer, but he did not fit the modern times of Facebook, cell phones, and streaming television. The decor of the trailer also fit his appearance. Well worn, practical, made for utility, with no extra frills.

Silas Buchanan had the hands of a working man. Rough and calloused. Most people would think he had worked construction or done farm work of some sort, but hardly anyone would guess he had spent most of his twenty plus years in law enforcement behind a desk. After his eventual and seemingly inevitable forced retirement from the police department, he had moved a day's drive away from Wichita, and opened his own private investigation firm out in farm country where the air was clean, roads were mostly free of traffic, and the cases he caught mostly consisted of hunting down stolen farm equipment or pulling husbands out of places they shouldn't be.

He wasn't from the country, though he felt more comfortable here, among the farmers-the men and women who made a living from the earth and the animals that roamed it. Silas had actually grown up in cities. St. Louis until he was twelve, and then Wichita until recently.

He had rented the trailer for a year, but eventually bought it from the owner, along with the other trailers scattered across the mobile home park around him. Renting them out brought him some steady money, but not much. The expenses often piled up faster than the rent. Over the years, tenants had come and gone. He used a few of the trailers to trade for work. A tow truck operator who gave him a hand from time to time lived in a double-wide at the back. An electrician lived in the middle of the lot. His room-mate paid rent with money. The electrician paid rent by working on all the other trailers. He also had a handyman and a landscaper living on the lot as well. Silas had been looking for a homeless plumber for years but plumbers rarely had the financial or addiction problems that other tradesmen seemed to have. At least in Silas' dealings, that had proven to be true. So he had to settle for paying plumbers cash until he found one that was down on his luck. At first appearance or hearing about his business practices second hand, it would be easy for someone to assume Silas was taking advantage of people, but in reality, trading them a place to stay in exchange for their skills and labor was actually mutually beneficial. If it wasn't, for either side, Silas ended the agreement. He had watched his father be taken advantage of all of his life, and he certainly wasn't out to champion that tendency. By providing a decent place to live to people who usually had to fight to keep themselves and their families at the same address for more than a year or two, Silas was able to present opportunities to people who rarely got them. In exchange, he received skills and labor that kept the trailers nice enough for people to be proud to live in them.

The answering machine played two messages that he cut off before they had barely started. Bill collectors. The third message was the one left just a few moments earlier, and Silas shook his head when the voice was cut off with a beep. "They always get nervous and talk too much," he said as he laid out the envelopes he had carried in from the mail box, separating out several with Past Due stamped on them. Those he put in a drawer.

From the back of the trailer, a dog walked up to meet him and sniff his work boots. "There you are old man," he said to the rottweiler who was more hound than rott, but had enough of that rottweiler face to pass for one. Rottweilers were more intimidating than hounds, so that's what Silas made everyone on the lot believe he was. A hound could make a lot of noise, but beyond that, they weren't known for instilling fear like Rotts were.

Silas walked into the kitchen area of the trailer and lifted the tight lid of the metal trash can which sat next to the plastic trash can. The plastic can was for trash. The metal one held the dog food. "Have at it," Silas said as he dumped a heaping scoop of the brown pellets into a bowl on the floor. After bending down and retrieving the other bowl, Silas filled it with water from the tap and set that bowl down next to the one the dog was already eating from. "Enjoy it, Pete." The dog had already been named Pete when Silas got him. A young family moved out of one of the trailers a few years earlier and left behind their dog along with a note from the son. The dog had looked starved at the time, and not just for food. "Somebody please take care of Pete," the note said, in a child's handwriting. Silas had read the note in silence, and then, with a click of his tongue, he signaled for the dog to follow him. Pete obeyed, and never went hungry again.

After Pete was fed, Silas reached for the white plastic bag he had carried in earlier. He opened up the tray of ground beef he took out of the bag and moved back over to the sink to wash his hands before forming the meat into patties. He left the meat on a plate on the table and walked out the back door which was at the end of a short hallway. Once outside, he retrieved a small bag of charcoal from a ledge underneath the trailer, emptied the rest of the bag into his red grill, dumped some lighter fluid on it, and lit it with his Zippo. The poofing sound followed by the singing of his right hand reminded him that he hadn't let the fluid soak into the charcoal long enough.

Once back inside, Silas sat down at his desk and replayed the only message left on the machine. He stared at the machine for a moment, and started to lift the receiver of the phone just as it started ringing. He smiled at how much it had startled him. "Hello?" he asked into the phone.

"Mr. Buchanan?" the voice on the other end asked.

"Yes sir," Silas said.

"My name is Larry Robertson. I called earlier."

"My machine cut you off. Sorry about that," Silas said.

"No worries," Larry said. "I was hoping I could talk to you about a problem I have. A question really."

"Is it a problem or a question?" Silas asked.

"Both," Larry said.

"Come on by Big Valley Acres." That's what Silas named the trailer park after he bought it. The park wasn't big, and it was at the dead end of an old trucking road, nowhere a valley of any sort. He named if after his favorite television show from when he was a kid. "Do you know where that is? A few miles past the bowling alley just inside the town limits. I'm assuming you're local."

"I used to be," Larry said. "I know where that is."

"I'm in lot 4A," Silas said. "The blue and white trailer near the flagpole."

"When?" Larry asked.

"Give me time to eat my supper," Silas said. "How about an hour from now?"

"Okay," Larry said. "I'll see you then. Thank you. In an hour. Thank you."

"Damn, he's awkward," Silas said out loud after hanging up the phone. "He must be young. Young ones are as awkward as hell these days."

Silas stood slowly, letting the kinks in his back work themselves out as he straightened up. Despite being tired already from a long day, he picked up his pace, went back to his bedroom, and returned to his desk carrying a shotgun. A quick movement of the drapes behind the desk and the gun was concealed within reach of his old orange chair.

Once he had taken the burgers outside and put them on the grill, Silas walked over to a trailer with an orange and brown stripe running down the side. After knocking on the front door, he walked around to the back and waited at the corner nearest the back door. Silas reached for his pack of Camels but left them in his pocket when he heard the sound of the door opening. A man moved slowly down the deck steps and began to walk quickly at a diagonal line away from the trailer. Silas stepped into his path after only a few steps.

When Silas put the palm of his hand out towards the man, he stopped. "I'm sorry Silas," he said. "I'll have it on Friday. I'm doing a job over in Lewiston, and he's gonna pay me cash."

"I'll wait until Friday, Tommy, if you're gonna have it all," Silas said.

"I'll have all of it," Tommy said. "I've just been in a bad place for a while."

"I get it," Silas said. "We all hit hard times. How about you show some good faith by hauling away the trash on the Bigelow lot?"

"They left already?" Tommy asked.

"Yeah," Silas said. "And they dumped all their trash in the yard on their way out."

"I'll grab it tomorrow," Tommy said.

"Thank you buddy." Silas hesitated, and then asked, "If I give you another week past Friday, can you round up enough cash to pay everything you owe?"

"Yes, sir," Tommy said quickly. "I definitely can do that."

"Great, see you then," Silas said as he walked back to his grill in time to grab the spatula hanging from the grill handle and flip the four burgers that were sizzling and dripping grease into the flames below. The smell began to draw some of the trailer park dogs, and Pete barked his disapproval from one of the windows.

Silas went back inside and re-emerged with a plate. While he waited for the burgers to finish, he smoked a camel and watched a few boys ride by on skateboards. One of the boys called over to him and he waved the hand that was holding the plate.

Once he had the burgers on the plate, Silas went back into the trailer and set his food on the table next to another white bag. At the refrigerator, he grabbed a small jar of mayonnaise, a big jar of pickles, and searched for the mustard. Not finding it, he grabbed the ketchup and set all of it on the table. After finally sitting down, he pulled a cold beer out of one of the white bags, opened the can and drank it slowly. After finishing it, he pulled another beer free from its plastic ring and opened it while pulling out hamburger buns from the other white bag. After building two impressive burgers with what he had grabbed from the refrigerator, He drank another beer while eating the first burger. He finished his third beer and started the fourth before eating his second burger. To Silas, there was no better burger than one cooked over charcoal.

By the time Larry Robertson knocked on his trailer door, Silas had finished off seven beers and four burgers. "Come on in," he shouted through the door, while moving over to his desk chair.

The man who walked through his door was barely a man. At least in appearance of age. To Silas, he seemed like he couldn't be more than a teenager on the verge of his twenties. "I'm here to see Silas

Buchanan," Larry said as he awkwardly stood in the area between the door and the desk.

"Have a seat Mr. Robertson," Silas said. "You found the place okay?"

"Yes," he said. "Well, I stopped at the wrong trailer first, but the lady living there pointed me over here to you, and she said to tell you she has pictures for you."

Silas nodded. "Good. Good." And then, because Larry had an odd look on his face, most likely thinking the pictures were something inappropriate, Silas added, "They're not sex pictures or anything. Well, they might be but not of her for me or of me. I mean, she helped me do a stakeout on a guy who's cheating on his wife with his boss."

"Oh, I see," Larry said. He shifted in his chair like it wasn't comfortable.

"So tell me what's going on, son," Silas said. He winced at himself for calling the boy, son, which did nothing but highlight how young he was, and how old Silas felt sitting across from him. Though he was probably only twenty-five years older, that still made him double the boy's age.

Larry shifted in his seat again and then began. "A month ago, my father's remains were pulled out of an old quarry south of town. He was in his wheelchair. At least, some of him was."

"I heard about that," Silas said. "I will most likely have some specific questions later, but I won't make you go through all of that yet. Jump to the problem. Then I might ask you to work backwards a bit in the narrative. I remember enough of the news stories to know what you're referring to so far."

Larry nodded and sat for a few moments, almost as if he had practiced what he was going to say and now had to figure out his next words. "I was his sole heir."

"He owned the quarry they found him in, right?" Silas asked quickly.

"No," Larry said. "His father did."

"I see," Silas said. "So your father was found in one of his father's quarries."

"Correct," Larry said.

"I don't remember anyone being arrested for it or charged."

"That's because no one ever was," Larry said. "The police ruled it a suicide."

"And you disagree with that," Silas said.

"I do."

"Do you think there was more to it?" Silas asked.

"I do. I think it was murder."

"And you want me to help you prove that?" Silas asked slowly. He lifted up his pack of Camels and shook one out. As he started to light it, he saw the look on Larry's face and asked, "You okay if I smoke?"

"I'd rather you not," Larry said. "Allergies."

Silas nodded and fiddled with the cigarette. "Tell me why you think your father was murdered."

"Several things point to murder and away from suicide. First of all, he was a paraplegic and confined to that wheelchair. Had been for over a year before he died."

"That would be a reason to take your own life," Silas said. "People get depressed for a lot less."

"Right," Larry said. "But one of the rednecks who pulled his remains out of the water told the police that he was tied to the wheelchair."

"Oh," Silas said. "That's odd."

"Yes," Larry said. "He was wrapped and tied with wire."

"Oh," Silas said. "What else?"

"And the police never found his van anywhere near the quarry."

"His van? Could he drive?"

"Yes," Larry said. "A man from his church customized it for him so he could drive it with his hands, including the accelerator and brake."

"And where is his van now?"

"Like I said. It was never found."

"Damn," Silas said. He sat for a moment, staring at his desk. Finally, he looked up. "And it's a cold case?"

"No," Larry said. "It's a closed case now."

"Okay," Silas said. "For me, that's a good thing. I won't investigate an open case. It has to be considered cold or closed. Why is this case closed? It should be cold."

"What's the difference?"

"Well, in a nutshell, cold means it is still technically open but no one is doing anything to investigate it any further. It's basically closed, but ready to reopen if new evidence re-emerges. Closed means they've either solved it or proclaimed it unsolvable for some reason. This doesn't sound like it should be a closed case."

"Do you ever investigate closed cases?"

"Sure, but with closed cases, it's more like I'm reinvestigating the case. Like if a family member wants me to prove their son or daughter was innocent of some crime they've been accused of."

"The police are calling it closed because they ruled it a suicide."

"Well," Silas said. "That's where I will start. Looking at whether or not it was one."

"It wasn't," Larry said. "I found someone. Well, some…thing, that had the motive to kill my father."

"Some thing?"

"Yes," Larry said. "He had land and some money from my grandfather. An antique car. Stuff like that. He left it all to a church."

"Oh," Silas said. "What does all of that add up to?"

"A hundred grand, maybe?" Silas said.

"You think a church would kill your father for a hundred grand worth of land and some cash and a car?"

"No," Larry said. "But they might for all the stock he holds in my grandfather's business."

"How much is that stock worth?" Silas asked.

"Over five million," Larry said.

Silas whistled. "Damn, son. How much of that did he leave you?"

"None of it," Larry said. "I got nothing."

"Are you doing this out of anger? Of course that's understandable if you are, but understanding your motivation for hiring me will help me know if I can meet your expectations."

"Am I angry? Sure. I'm angry. At my father, because all he ever did was give everything to churches. All my life. The churches may have changed, but it was always the same. He gave all of his time to them. I never saw him, because he was always away from home. He gave all of our money to them, too. Do you know how many times I saw my father put money in an offering plate when he couldn't even put food on our plates at home? More times than I can count. And I'm mad at the church for always taking advantage of him. All the way up until his death. Always taking, taking, and taking. So yeah, I'm mad. And I want you to prove this church killed him.

"What's the name of the church?" Silas asked, reaching for his notebook and a pen.

"Wren River Baptist Church."

Larry's cell phone rang and when he saw Silas wince, he quickly touched the screen to ignore it. "Sorry."

Silas held the cigarette still in his fingers and then began to twirl it. "You said you think the church was responsible for your father's death, but the whole church didn't kill him. Do you have any specific person in mind?."

"I don't know. The preacher? That's who I would start with."

"I'm gonna grab a beer," Silas said. "Can I get you something?"

"Do you have bottled water?"

"I've got tap water," Silas said. "Sorry about that. But it's well water. It's really good well water."

"I'm fine," Larry said. He sat silently while Silas grabbed one beer and then a second and third before returning to the desk. Larry looked at him for a moment and then continued.

Silas drank the rest of his beer and slowly felt the buzz of it run across his body and into his mind. He blinked a few times and sat up in his chair. "Son, do you want answers, or just money?"

"There is no such thing as, "just money", Mr. Buchanan," Larry said. "It's all that matters now. My father is gone. I can't get him back. I just need the money so this doesn't ruin the rest of my life. It's my money, and this church has it. And I want it back. It's as simple as that. I can't even finish college now."

"You could work and go to school at the same time," Silas said. That's what his daughter was doing. He wanted to like this kid, find some way to relate to him, but right now he seemed like a thirsty man who stood out in the yard with an empty glass, waiting for it to rain.

"I do," Larry said. "I'm trying to graduate without loans...or help from my grandfather. And I've just gone underwater a bit. The bills come in faster than the paychecks."

Well, that was something Silas could relate to. He opened another can of beer and drank it quicker than he had planned. While he did, his mind went to the piles of bills in his drawer. "I'll help," Silas said. "Here are my rates, and a contract I'm gonna need you to sign. I need five hundred dollars up front as a portion of my fee. I also need another five hundred to cover any expenses I might encounter. If I exhaust that, I will call you for more. I save receipts and keep a little ledger sheet I will give you when all of this is over."

"Fair enough," Larry said, reaching for the contract. He signed it without reading it and passed it back to Silas. "What else do you need to know?"

Silas noted that he didn't ask about the hourly rate. "Keep in mind, if I prove it was a suicide, I still get paid."

"You won't find it was suicide," Larry said. "But I understand."

Silas nodded. "I need any contact information you have on the church and the name of the pastor. How much investigating have you done on your own, son?"

"None," Larry said. "I tried, but they don't even have a website or social media pages. Why do you ask?"

"Okay," Silas said as he stood up. "I'll take over from here. That's all I need for now, Mr. Robertson. I'll call you with an update in a couple of days, a week at the most." He calculated the fee, and looked towards the drawer where he kept the bills. He needed to solve this one quickly and get paid quickly. A feeling of guilt hit him for approaching the case like that, but the bills were a reality, and as long as the kid got a true result, it didn't really matter how quickly he solved the case. This went against the way he was trained to do police work, but he reminded himself that he wasn't police anymore.

"Okay," Larry said. He stood up quickly like he was suddenly in a hurry to leave, which was fine by Silas. "Wait. How do I get the money to you?" he asked. "Do you have Venmo? Paypal?"

"Just bring it by tomorrow morning," Silas said.

Larry nodded his head in agreement. What time?"

"How about eight?" Silas felt the room spin just a bit faster than normal. "Better make it eight-thirty."

As they walked to the door together, Larry turned and shook his hand. "Thank you for taking this case," Larry said. "It means a lot to me."

Silas nodded and as Larry walked to his car in the glow of the outdoor lights, Silas called out to him. "Be careful going home." He wasn't sure why he said that. It just came out.

Larry turned, looked like he was about to say something, but instead just nodded, waved, and got into his car. As he drove away, Silas could hear the gravel popping under the tires of the old Ford Escort. Not unlike most of his clients, Larry seemed to be only telling part of the story. Either way, he was a client, and Silas needed clients as much as Larry needed him.

Across the park, a rooster crowed. Silas squinted into the darkness. "Who the hell is raising chickens around here?"

Chapter 2

Silas was dreaming someone was knocking on his door when he realized someone really was knocking. That same someone was also shouting his name. The sounds were coming from right outside his bedroom, at the rear door. He moved himself slowly out of bed and looked for his shotgun. It was out by the desk. He cursed himself for forgetting it as he pulled on his pants and boots. He looked around for his shirt but whoever it was at his door was now thumping it like they were slamming something against it. "I'm on my way!" he shouted as he crouched and ran quickly past the rear door. A small rectangular piece of frosted glass was at the top of the door, but it wouldn't let him see who was on the other side. When he reached the living room, Silas grabbed a small revolver from the top drawer of his desk and then threw open the front door. No one was there. He made a grunting sound as he tried to wake up his legs. They moved slow in the mornings. His right leg was the reason he was forced to retire. At least that's what he told people. The real reason had more to do with his trigger finger than his leg.

Silas walked around the trailer and moved enough of his head past the rear corner to see who was knocking on his door. "Dammit, Tommy," Silas said, lowering his pistol and slipping it into his back pocket. "What the hell is going on?"

"There was a man over at my trailer asking about you," Tommy said.

"What kind of questions was he asking?" Silas tried to push through the fog that had settled over his mind.

"He asked who owned your trailer. I was sitting out on my porch this morning. Just got home from work. Side jobs. You know. And I guess he stopped to ask me because I was the only person out and around awake."

"What time?"

"Five? No. Closer to six. I got off at five."

"He was asking who lived in my trailer?"

"Yeah. I said I didn't know."

"Did he use my name?" Silas asked as he looked around the trailer park.

"Nice shirt, Silas!" a woman called as she drove by.

"Hey Shelly," Silas waved and self consciously crossed his arms, before turning back to Tommy. "Did anyone use my name?"

"No," Tommy said. "But he was acting strange. And there were like three other guys waiting in the car for him while he talked to me. I couldn't see them clearly enough. It wasn't full daylight yet."

"Thanks for the heads up, Tommy," Silas said. "I appreciate it."

"I got a license plate," Tommy said, with a smile.

"Bullshit," Silas said with a laugh. "Tell me you're serious."

"I'm dead ass serious," Tommy said. He handed Silas a piece of paper with the license plate number on it. "It was a Subaru Outback. I remember noticing because usually only lesbians drive those cars."

Silas shook his head. "You can't talk like that anymore, Tommy. It'll get you into trouble."

"Not if I meant it as a compliment. They've got good taste in cars. That's all I'm saying," Tommy said, with his hands held out away from his body. "Just like it ain't racist if it's a compliment. I'm a black man. Compliment me. Compliment my race," Tommy said. "I ain't gonna complain."

"Times are changing, my friend." Silas extended his hand. "I appreciate this," he said, as he held up the piece of paper.

"Don't mention it," Tommy said.

"Hey," Silas said. "If you need a few more days to pay rent, just let me know."

"Nah," Tommy said. "I'll have it to you even quicker than I thought. Like I said."

"Thank you, Tommy," Silas said as he shook his hand. "I'm sorry I came at you so hard about the rent. I've just got bill collectors swarming me lately. But then I did the same thing to you. Swarm you, I mean, collecting bills."

"It's the circle of lower middle class life," Tommy said, with a laugh.

"If they come back again," Silas said, ring me up please."

"You need a cell," Tommy said.

"Someday maybe," Silas said. "I'm not even fifty yet."

"You're almost fifty."

"Yeah. I'll get one eventually."

"By then, we'll be flying around in space ships," Tommy said.

"You never know," Silas said, as he walked back to his trailer. When he got to the back deck he noticed boot prints in the dirt. They were all across the back of the trailer, but Silas couldn't track them on the sides or front, where the grass was actually growing. He looked around and across the park before going back inside. The time surprised him when he looked at the clock. It was almost eight. He must have been dead asleep when whoever it was came to check out the trailer. Before sitting down in his chair, Silas moved the pistol from his pocket to the top drawer of the desk. He reached behind the curtains and moved the shotgun closer so he could grab it quicker when necessary.

Silas lit a cigarette as he picked up the phone receiver and dialed a number by memory. "Hey Demi, it's Silas. How ya been?" He took a drag on the cigarette and listened. "Good. Can I trouble you for a rundown?" Another drag and a long exhale. "DYZ 17A2." As he listened, he scrambled to reach for his notebook. "I'm ready. Got it. Demi I owe you one. Tell that slack ass husband of yours hello for me." As he hung up the phone, Silas moved quickly back to his bedroom and grabbed a shirt. Slipping it on, he opened up his closet and pulled out another pistol. This one was a revolver like the other one, but packed more of a punch. He preferred revolvers, even though he knew it made him look like an antique.

Once he grabbed his keys, Silas took another look around the trailer and then remembered Larry was coming by within the hour. He walked quickly to the phone and dialed Larry's number. It went straight to voicemail, so Silas left a message that he would come by Larry's house for the money instead of Larry coming by the trailer.

The town of Wren River was unincorporated and relied upon the nearby towns for its malls and movie theaters and chain restaurants. Silas tried to stay closer to Wren River because he had grown tired of being around large groups of people. As he drove, Silas decided to check out the address the Outback was registered to before going to Larry's house. It was just outside of town and only took him fifteen minutes to get there. He rode by quickly at first just to get a quick look. It was a small ranch style brick house. No vehicles parked out front. There was no garage attached. He turned his truck around and made another pass. All the blinds on the front were down.

Silas made two quick lefts and drove along the block behind the house. All he could see was that the backyard was fenced in by a high wooden fence. No more to see or do here until later, after the sun went down. He headed towards the highway, and smoked a cigarette on his way to Larry's house. The realization that he hadn't had coffee yet came across his mind and he made a quick stop at a gas station to grab a cup. While he drove he sipped the hot coffee and smiled to himself. Most people guessed he took his coffee black, but his best kept secret was that he loved the amaretto cream. Lots of it. He tried black coffee once and gagged on it. He liked the fact that he fit the image of a black coffee guy but he liked his coffee the color of his cigarette filters.

Silas steered with one hand while he finished his coffee and parked in front of Larry's house. It was a nice split level in a nice neighborhood outside of Wren River town limits. Most of the nice places in the area happened to be outside of town. This house was particularly nice. Did he live at home with his mother? This didn't look like a single guy's house. Once he got to the door, Silas rang the doorbell and stepped back down to the first step. He hated when people rang or knocked and then stood all close to the door. He liked to give people some space when they opened the door. As a private investigator, he found that it came across as less intimidating. Coming across as kind and unimposing was far more effective than throwing his weight around or raising his voice. He could do it when he needed to, but he saw way too much of that on the force, and it didn't take him long to come to the conclusion that it rarely worked.

When the door opened, a woman stood there looking confused. "May I help you?" she asked.

So maybe he did live with his mother. "Is Larry home?" Silas asked.

"Larry?" Her initial look of confusion turned into suspicion as she took a step back from the doorway. "No one named Larry lives here. I live here with my husband," she said. "He will be home in a few minutes."

"Is this the Robertson residence?" Silas asked. He also took a step backwards.

"It's not," she said. She didn't slam the door, but she closed it quickly and the next sound he heard was the deadbolt clicking into place.

As Silas drove away, he dialed the number Larry gave him and it went straight to voicemail again. Fake address. Possible fake phone number. It made no sense. Instead of driving home, he turned towards the downtown area and a few minutes later, he was parked on main street in front of the police station. After his revolver was locked in the glove compartment, he crossed the street and went inside.

Chapter 3

The Police Department lobby was small and surprisingly empty. Behind a counter, protected by a glass partition, was a tall and thin lady who appeared to be in her mid-thirties. "What can I help you with?" she asked through a microphone. Her voice came out of a speaker mounted on the lobby side of the counter.

"Hello, Officer...," Silas leaned forward to read her name tag. "Ellen. Officer Ellen."

"I'm not an officer," she said bluntly but still politely. "I'm a civil servant."

"Well alrighty, Civil Servant Ellen. I was hoping to see one of your detectives. I'm a local private investigator." He held his license up to the glass.

"Is there a particular Detective you want to see, sir?" she asked, flatly.

Silas smiled to himself. Civil Servant Ellen had the emotions of a lunch sack. "Well, do you have a Detective who is assigned to the closed cases?"

"That's not how it works," she said. "Closed cases are closed."

Silas forced a smile. "Of course. So does the original Detective who was assigned to the case stay assigned to the closed case?"

"That's now how it works," she repeated dryly. "Closed cases are–"

"Closed. I get it. Let's start over. Who would I talk to about a closed case?"

"Take a seat," she said without looking at him. Her left hand pointed towards three chairs by the front door while she opened a door behind her with her right hand.

After she disappeared behind the door, Silas made a conscious effort to keep his temper under control as he sat down in the chair furthest from the door. After a few minutes passed, a police officer walked in and cut through the lobby quickly before going through a door Silas hadn't noticed. Several minutes after that, a different officer came out of that door and went through the door leading back outside. More time passed, and an older woman came in from outside, walked to the counter, and pushed a buzzer. Civil Servant Ellen walked up to the counter and spoke through the speaker. "May I help you?" she asked.

The woman told Ellen all of her troubles, and was promptly directed to sit by the door. Silas stood up as the lady sat down. He walked quickly to the counter and spoke through the glass. "Excuse me. I'm sorry. Is someone coming to speak to me?"

"What case are you here about?" Ellen asked.

Silas laughed. He didn't even try to stifle it. "The closed case. You were getting a detective for me to speak with about a closed case."

Ellen just stared at him. "What was the victim's name? Do you know it?"

"Tucker Robertson," Silas said.

Her stare blipped for a second. That's the best way Silas could describe it. When he was growing up, television signals came through a roof antenna, and every now and then, the picture would go out for a second, and his parents called those moments, "blips". That's what happened to Civil Servant Ellen when he said Tucker Robertson's name. She blipped. Only for a second. And then she said, "You will need to see Sergeant Mesa." With that, she turned around and left again through the same door.

Silas didn't have to wait long at the window before a tall officer came through the door and introduced himself as the desk Sergeant. He led Silas to an empty room and said that Sergeant Mesa would be with him shortly.

After almost thirty minutes of waiting, the Sergeant came in, introduced himself, and proceeded to tell Silas that the case was closed and ruled a suicide. Even after asking a string of questions, Silas felt like he was getting no answers in return.

The Sergeant looked too young to be as tired as he appeared or as frustrated as he seemed. "I don't know what else to tell you. We ruled it a suicide. Pretty cut and dry. The old man was deep in debt. His family had cut him off. He was a paraplegic. So he rolls himself off the dock and drowns himself."

"I'm under the impression he was tied to the chair," Silas said.

"He was. He tied himself to it so he couldn't swim free."

"He was paralyzed from the waist down. How could he swim free?" Silas asked.

"He could still use his arms," the Sergeant said. "Most people in wheelchairs have strong arms. We came to the conclusion that he tied himself to the chair and rolled himself into the water."

Silas sat at the table for a moment. He could tell that any other questions he asked would get the same type of dismissive response. These guys had purposefully closed this case and no one was going to be allowed to question whether or not it should be otherwise. "Thank you for your time Sergeant Mesa," Silas said as he stood up and walked to the door.

"Glad to help," the Sergeant said.

Silas couldn't even stifle the laugh before it escaped his mouth. "If I have any more questions about this case, I'm assuming I should contact you?"

"Correct," the Sergeant said.

Silas started to make a sarcastic comment but instead, he left the room, walked across the police station lobby, waved at Civil Servant Ellen, and exited into a downpour. He couldn't help but smile at how quickly this promising day had turned sour.

Inside the truck, Silas let the water run down his face. He tried to wipe it with the sleeve of his shirt, but it was soaked and did nothing but move the water around. Shaking his head like a dog, he watched the water droplets fly around the cab of the truck. In the middle of June, the temperature outside seemed like it had dropped twenty degrees but he knew it hadn't. It was just the combination of the wind and rain making him cold. It was temporary. If he had learned anything over his fifty years, it was that everything, both the good and the bad, is temporary. Right now he had no money to pay his bills, but that was temporary. He had a case that looked like it was going nowhere, but that was temporary.

"The question you need to answer, Silas, is this," he said out loud to himself. "Do you need a client in order to have a case?" He took time to think about that question for a while. The rain had stopped, so he stepped out of the truck and felt the fresh air on his face. His clothes would start drying. The wet would become damp and the damp would become dry. "Do you need a client in order to have a case?" he repeated. "No." He knew he did not. So now he was left with the thing he had known for a long time about the temporal state of the world. He had a case to solve. More specifically, he had a case that right now was closed. Since this was his case, it was his job to make sure the closed status of this case was just temporary. The question of how he would get paid came into his mind and refused to leave. Silas forced himself to ignore it.

"Time to get to work, Silas," he said, as he climbed back into the truck, reached across to the glove compartment, grabbed his revolver, holstered it, and pulled out a map from the driver's side visor. A few minutes later he was driving towards Wren River Baptist Church.

Chapter 4

The cross on top of the steeple was visible above the treeline before he saw the church. The "End of State Maintenance" sign was at least a mile back, so by the time he rounded the curve and saw the little brick building, Silas knew he had found what he was looking for even before he spotted the sign near the woods that said, "Welcome To Wren River Baptist Church". It was white with black lettering.

There were two cars parked in the small lot, and Silas pulled into the space between a small truck and a minivan. There was a door on the side of the building, and a set of double doors at the top of a small set of steps at the front of the church. He decided to try the side door and as he neared it, he saw the Office sign and when he tried the knob it turned and opened. On the other side of the door was a small room. In the middle of the room was a ladder. At the top of the ladder was a man who appeared to be installing a ceiling fan. He was dressed in work clothes-the dark blue type that they sell at places called "The Working Man's Store" or somewhere like that. As the door clicked closed, he looked down and smiled. "Hello there," the man said. "Can I help you?"

"Yes," Silas said. "I sure hope so. I guess I'm looking for the man in charge."

"You mean God?" the man said from the top of the ladder. "If so, you came to the right place."

Silas didn't know what to say at first, so he just laughed. The man on the ladder smiled and climbed down, leaving his tools on the top of the ladder. "I'm Bob Parks," the man said with another smile. "If you're looking for the person in charge of this place, most of the gossipers would say you were looking for my wife. The congregation would say you're looking for Beverly, our church secretary. But I'm the pastor here, so you're most likely looking for me."

"Oh," Silas said, not doing a good job at hiding his surprise. He wasn't dressed the way he expected a pastor to dress. No bow tie or cardigan sweater. "Yes. You're exactly who I'm looking for."

Once they were both seated in the pastor's office, Silas decided to approach this head on, instead of beating around the bush, which was how most private investigators seemed to operate. "Mr. Parks, my name is Silas Buchanan. I've been hired to investigate, or I guess you would say, re-investigate the death of Tucker Robertson. You're familiar with Mr. Robertson? You knew him?"

"Of course," he said. The pastor turned in his chair and opened up a small file cabinet. After a moment, he withdrew a small folder and opened it up on his desk. "When he died, he left his estate to this church. But of course, I'm sure you knew that. That's why you're here. Did his father hire you?"

"No," Silas said. "But I can't reveal my client's identity. I'm sure you understand confidentiality, Mr. Parks."

"I do," he said. "And please call me Bob. Since Tuck is no longer with us, I can speak freely about him without fear of breaking confidentiality, but if you're here to find a reason to sue us, maybe I need to be careful what I say."

"You only need to be careful if what you say will incriminate you and make me think you murdered him or that you know who did," Silas said.

"Ah," Bob said as he nodded. "You think he was murdered. Or at least your client does."

"Maybe," Silas said. "Would that surprise you?"

"No, it would not."

"Really? Why not?" Silas asked. He reminded himself to slow down and listen. It was human tendency to ask a question and then spend time thinking about the next question without listening to the answer. Silas had trained himself to ask questions that would produce answers worth listening to.

"How long have you been investigating this case Mr. Buchanan?" He looked down at the file and back up at Silas. "And I don't mean that as an insult. I'm not a passive aggressive person. I can be blunt sometimes, though."

"To tell you the truth, Bob, you're my first stop. I took the case last night around suppertime."

"Well," Bob said with a smile. "In light of Tuck's will, I have to admit if I were wearing your boots, I would be pointing them in this direction as well."

"I appreciate you understanding that." He found himself liking this man, which would complicate matters if it turned out that he was the killer. "So I guess I have to ask if you mind showing me that file you have there." He pointed at Bob's desk with a smile. "I'm assuming that's on Mr. Robertson."

"I'll make you a deal," Bob said. "If you agree to come back later in the week or early next week, to continue this interview or whatever it is, I will let you take this file home. And I have a video I would like you to watch. I'm assuming you have a DVD player?"

"That would be a bad assumption, Bob," Silas said. "But I can find someone who will let me use theirs."

"Good," Bob said. "Then I will give you this file, and a DVD for you to watch. After you do, I believe you will have some other interviews that will overshadow me as a priority. But I will be here whenever you're ready to return and follow up."

"You've got a deal, Pastor," Silas said without realizing why he used the man's official title.

After a quick tour of the church, Bob left Silas in the big room that he called the sanctuary while he climbed a ladder up to a small room that opened up and functioned as a sound room. There was a camera peaking over a railing and various microphones extending from the room, along with wires leading off in various directions across the ceiling.

When he came back down, Bob was holding a clear plastic package. "Here's the DVD I told you about," Bob said, extending it towards Silas. Written on the cover in black magic marker were the words, "Tucker Robertson-Testimony".

After confirming he would be back soon with more questions, Silas drove back to the highway and took the road leading home. It took him less than twenty minutes to get there, but by the time he pulled into the trailer lot, his stomach was telling him to stop and eat. He rounded the trailer twice before stopping at the edge of the woods to the rear of the lot. It was just a quick walk from this truck to the trailer, but it hid the truck enough for him to know he could approach the trailer safely in case anyone was waiting. He took his time approaching and entering the trailer and when he was certain no one was inside, he went into the kitchen and made a bologna sandwich with mayo and just a quick shot of mustard. Silas used the bologna to spread the little bit of mustard across the bread before putting the sandwich together and eating it in just a few bites. Back at the refrigerator, he reached for a beer, but paused and chose the almost empty pitcher of sweet tea. After pouring himself a glass, he made another sandwich similar to the first one, except he added a handful of chips on top of the bologna before squishing the two slices of bread together.

He finished his lunch while flipping through the file on Tucker Robertson. It didn't contain much. A copy of the cover letter for the will. The actual copy of the will wasn't in the file. A few letters back and forth between the lawyers. The file was thin. A visitor card he filled out. A request for visitation at the hospital. A few certificates for Bible Study classes. A baptism certificate was at the back of the file, along with a picture of Tucker being baptized in his wheelchair. The irony of the photo was not lost on Silas who made a "hmph" sound and shook his head slowly. The last piece of paper in the file was the only helpful document in there. It was a short letter from Tucker to the pastor.

Silas read the middle paragraph twice. It said, "You asked the other day if this was the first church I belonged to, and I said yes, but that was a lie, Pastor, and I am sorry. I belonged to a traveling tent church for almost twenty years. I am not proud of what I did while part of that church. We were all frauds. So when I told you I was never a member of any other church, I thought I was telling the truth, technically, but as you taught this morning, holding back even a part of the truth, is the same as telling a lie. I have made my repentance and peace with the past, but I didn't want to build our relationship on a lie."

He went on to ask forgiveness again and to thank the Pastor for accepting him for who he was. Silas looked back through the file again, and then grabbed the DVD and a pack of cigarettes. He called out for Pete, and he came running from the back. "Good boy," Silas said. "Take a walk with me."

As Silas and Pete crossed the trailer park, another rain cloud passed over and it began to sprinkle just as they arrived at a nice double-wide in the middle of the park. It was white with green trim. The front yard area was filled with small patches of flowers. When the door opened, Silas said, "Hey. Hello. Can we come in for just a minute Jenny?"

Jenny spoke over her shoulder. "You girls head on to the other trailer. I've got company." She turned back to Silas. "You're always welcome here, Sugar. Come on in.

Once inside, Pete went towards the back of the trailer where the voices of several women welcomed him.

"What do you need, Silas?" Jenny asked as she walked towards the kitchen. "Follow me. I was just making some tea. Want some?"

"Hot or cold?" Silas asked.

"Hot," Jenny answered.

"I'll pass, but thank you Jenny."

"What brings you by?" Jenny asked as she sipped from a tiny white tea cup.

"I was hoping I could borrow your DVD player for a minute. Didn't you have a mobile one? For your car? Or am I thinking of someone else?"

"You came to the right place," Jenny said. "I actually have one I let my grandson use. You wanna borrow it? It's easy to use." She moved over to the entertainment center and started opening drawers.

"I would be obliged," Silas said. Not many women brought out his nervous side, but Jenny Mercer always could. "Can I bring it back later on today?"

"You can use it here if you want to," Jenny said. "It's raining outside."

"I don't wanna mess up your business," Silas said. "If you don't mind me borrowing it, I'll bring it back later on."

"You can only borrow it if you bring it back after dark," Jenny said with a smile as she handed the player to him.

Silas laughed and nodded. "Sounds good to me, Jenny." As he walked to the door with the small DVD player, he turned around and gave her a quick hug. "Thanks again," he said. "I owe you one."

"You sure do," she said as Pete emerged from the back and followed Silas down the front porch and across the trailer park.

As they neared the back of the trailer, Pete began barking and ran to the edge of the back deck, barking and growling. "What do you see, boy?" Silas called out. The dog growled louder and ran up under the trailer where he began to bark and growl. Suddenly he began to make noise like he was attacking something or someone. "Pete?" Silas called out.

A man began to curse and yell from somewhere under the trailer and as Silas drew his revolver, he felt pain shoot through his head from the front to the back, and then darkness.

A voice in the distance was calling out his name, but he needed more sleep. His pillow must have fallen off of the bed. He tried to reach for it but his arm wouldn't obey his mind. His bed was hard and his pillow felt like dirt. He needed more sleep and he wouldn't get it without his pillow, so he made himself sit up to look for it. The voice in the distance would have to wait.

After more darkness for more time, the voice came again. This time it wasn't from so far away. "Be careful, Silas," Tommy said. "You took a bad hit, bro."

Silas heard his own voice answering Tommy and then he felt the big man lift him. His feet dragging against the gravel. It sounded like when he was a kid, dragging a stick along, pretending it was a horse. He would ride it across the grass and along the driveway. The sound was oddly comforting and he fell back down into the blackness.

The stucco on his ceiling looked like icicles. He had never noticed that before today. Silas squinted to see the stucco patterns more clearly, but his vision kept blurring, and his head hurt when he tried to focus. He made the clicking sound to call Pete, but Tommy appeared instead.

"Why am I on the couch?" Silas asked.

"You're not making sense, buddy," Tommy said. "Take your time."

Silas stared at Tommy and then tried asking again. "Why am I on the couch?"

"I know you think you're making sense," Tommy said. "But you're not. I'm sorry."

Silas felt the room move a bit so he closed his eyes and tried to sit up. Time passed, but he didn't know how much. After a while, he tried again. "What happened?" He opened his eyes and Tommy was across the room in a chair, asleep. Jenny was sitting on the floor.

She turned around slowly and smiled. "You're awake," she said. "We were about to take you to the hospital, but you weren't bleeding and Tommy said with your line of work, maybe you wouldn't want us to."

"I'm allowed to go to the hospital in my line of work," Silas said with what he hoped was a smile. "But Tommy probably knows I wouldn't want the bill." Silas reached for his cigarettes and shook one out. His lighter was gone. Jenny reached over and lit it with her disposable.

"What the hell happened?" Jenny asked. "Tommy came along and you were half in a mud puddle and half in the gravel."

"Shit!" Silas said suddenly. "Did I drop your DVD player?"

"It was in the yard," she said with the same smile. "Don't worry. It still works, I'm sure."

Silas nodded and asked, "What about the DVD? Do you know if that's gone?"

"Tommy didn't say anything about a DVD." Her smile faded and she was quiet for too long. "Silas, I gotta tell you something."

"Just tell me," Silas said. His mind was moving back and forth in time and he knew what she was going to say just before she finally said it.

"Pete is dead. Tommy found him under the trailer."

Silas stared at her for a long time and then finally said, "I'm okay." It was a lie, but he didn't know what else to say. The weight of it hit him and he felt his eyes grow hot and then wet. He tried to say something else, but didn't trust himself not to break down and when it was all said and done, it wasn't fair to Jenny to be vulnerable one minute and emotionally unavailable the next. Instead, he handed Jenny his cigarette, laid back down and closed his eyes so tight they hurt. Sleep came again and when he woke up later, the trailer was dark.He stood up and walked by memory to the kitchen and found the light switch. He turned around after the lights came on and saw Tommy awake in the chair. Silas raised a hand and Tommy raised one back. He was hungry so he made a sandwich from peanut butter. It was the easiest thing to make. He ate it too quickly and found a beer, opened it, and drained it. He slowly made his way back to the living room and sat down heavily on the couch. After a long moment, he said. "I owe you one, chief."

Tommy smiled from the dimly lit corner and said, "I watched your TV all day and smoked your Camels, drank your liquor, and ate your food. I'd say we're even."

Silas smiled. He ran his hand up his neck and felt a sensitive area. Further up the back of his head, he found the knot, and winced at the stabbing pain his touch caused. He felt around the rest of his head and felt one wet spot. Moving his hand away, he looked at it and saw a bit of blood. Not much. Not enough to worry about.

"You didn't happen to see who did this, by any chance?"

"Nope," Tommy said. "But I found this." He picked up a denim jacket from the floor and tossed it to Silas. "Look in the pocket."

Silas felt around the jacket, found the pocket, and pulled out a wallet. For the first time in what had to have been several hours, Silas smiled. He opened the wallet and found cash and an ID. He checked the ID for an address and realized it was just a few miles away. He counted the cash. Four hundred dollars. Silas pulled out the cash and leaned over, hand outstretched towards Tommy. "Take it," he said.

Tommy slowly reached forward, took the money, and shoved it slowly into his pocket. "You sure?" he asked.

"Oh, yeah," Silas said. He held up the wallet. "You earned every dollar."

"I'm sorry about Pete," Tommy said.

"Where is he?" Silas asked.

"I buried him," Tommy said. "It was hot out. I didn't--"

"Thank you," Silas said quickly. "You did the right thing." After a long pause, he felt like he should say more, but he could only repeat himself. "Thank you."

Silas looked around at his clock, expecting it to tell him it was five o'clock in the evening, but instead it said nine thirty-five. It was night-time. Since the trailer was dark before he turned the lights on, that made sense. He tried to figure out what time it would have been when he was hit. Two o'clock maybe? He looked back over at Tommy, who was now asleep again. It took a bit of effort to stand up, but when he did, he didn't feel dizzy any longer. He stretched and felt better. After walking in small circles around the living room, Silas reached behind the curtain and grabbed hold of the shotgun. He reached into the desk drawer and retrieved his pistol.

Outside, the air was thick with heat. He thought it would be fresh and cool, but it was barely either. Being away from the stale air that one inevitably breathes in a room with walls and a floor and a ceiling, is what he needed, though. Silas made his way across the yard, using the faint light of the moon and his memory. About fifty feet from the trailer, near the edge of the woods was a picnic table he put there for the park families. None of them used it, though. The teenagers liked to hang out there, but that was mostly it. The position of it gave him an almost complete view of his trailer except for the back corner, which was the portion with no windows or doors. From there, he felt like he could rest and watch his home.

Sometime around midnight, Tommy emerged and disappeared in the darkness towards his trailer. A few minutes later, his truck started up. He was probably heading to work. He probably only got a few hours of sleep but he was a worker. It was one of many reasons why Silas gave him a break on rent most months. This month had been an exception only because income had been way down.

Sitting at the picnic table, Silas began to work his mind through everything that had happened over the past day and a half. He had a client who hired him but disappeared before paying. He had a man who may have been murdered, but the police say he killed himself. The person with the most to gain by the victim's death seemed nice and helpful. Sadly, Silas had been in law enforcement and investigation long enough to know, though, that nice and helpful really didn't mean a lot in the long run. Nice and helpful people had murdered their friends and families for ages.

As he slowly drank his beer, questions began to line up for attention. Who sent the guys to attack him? Were they connected to this case or one of his other ones? Did they come for the DVD or did they just take it to take it? Who sent them? It wouldn't make sense for Pastor Bob to send them. Who else knew he was on the case but Larry and the police?

As the questions piled up, and the answers stayed away, Silas decided to take the reins again. He hated not feeling in control. The shotgun ended up on the rack behind the truck seat, and his revolver stayed in his holster. When he started the big truck up, dogs across the park began to bark their complaints at the engine noise which had so rudely interrupted their sleep.

As he drove, Silas made some decisions. This case was certainly not going to provide a quick payoff to his bills. He could dump it, but he was in too deep to do that now, and the decent part of him, the part of him that wasn't motivated by getting creditors off his back, knew he needed to follow this investigation to the end. Solve the case. Help reveal the truth. Silas embraced that part of himself and decided to lean into this one. He now had two addresses in connection with people who had come to his home. The first address was through the license plate of the car driven by the man who was asking Tommy a bunch of questions. The second came from the wallet left behind by the men who knocked him out, and then killed Pete. He also needed to visit Wren River again. Surely they would have another copy of the DVD. His first inclination was to let the sun rise on him getting revenge for Pete. Instead, though, he pulled into the parking lot of a small diner, found Pastor Bob's card, and called him.

As they ate, all Silas could concentrate on was the fact that this man loved bacon. Lots of people love bacon. This was America after all. Even with all the diet crazes going on, bacon still managed to remain in the upper echelon of modern meat choices. But this man really loved bacon. He had a cup of coffee. Two pieces of toast. Eight slices of bacon. Grits with bacon broken up in it. A bacon biscuit. And an omelet with bacon and cheddar cheese. And the man was not overweight in stature. He was of average shape and size for a man who isn't necessarily fit, but wouldn't be considered out of shape.

In between bacon choices, Bob spoke. "When Tuck came to us, he was already in the wheelchair. Car accident out on the interstate one night. A few people died. He came out of it paralyzed from the waist down. One Sunday morning there he was, in the back of the church, sitting in the short row of chairs underneath the shelves where we stack the offering plates and beside the coat rack. Over time our church got to know him, and he got to know us and eventually he wanted to join. During the process of officially becoming a member of the church he began to allude to his past."

"Is that normal?" Silas asked as he sipped his coffee.

"Very," Bob said. "I can't tell you how many stories I've heard over the years about sordid pasts and regrets and such. But Tuck's story was different."

"In what way?" Silas asked.

"Well, first of all, everyone says they used to be a bad person, but Tucker Robertson really was a very bad person. I mean God can and will forgive everyone of anything, but Tuck," he laughed and ate a slice of bacon, "Tuck was a con man. Or as he told it, he was a shill for a con man."

"He worked for someone."

"Yes. I didn't know what shill meant, but he told me. There was this traveling church, and I use the word church lightly, because I don't think this was a church at all. They were a traveling con job. Tuck's job was to show up at these tent revivals across the country, in a wheelchair."

Silas raised his eyebrows and stopped mid-sip with his coffee. "A wheelchair?" he asked.

"Yep," Bob said. "Talk about irony, huh? Some people would say karma's a...you know."

"Yes they would," Silas said as he shook his head. "Damn."

"Right?" Bob asked. "So he would show up in a wheelchair and when the preacher, this guy, Bodean Culp, would start calling for anyone who needed healing, someone would roll Tucker Robertson to the front. And then when Culp would heal him after this big spectacle, Bob would jump out of the chair and run around the tent, healed."

"And the people would toss all kinds of money into the offering plate," Silas said.

"Oh, yes," Bob said. "Lots of money. And they did this from town to town for years."

"How many years?" Silas asked.

"Over ten," Bob said. "And of course they switched it up some. Bob wore disguises. Sometimes he was blind. But he was Culp's go to guy."

"So what ended it?" Silas asked.

Bob stopped with a big piece of bacon in mid-air and said, "The car accident, I think. I'm not really sure. I'm assuming when he got paralyzed for real. After that, they had no more use for him. They kicked him to the curb, I guess. He drank himself into a dark place. And then he came to us."

"And that's why he left everything to your church? Because you were there for him when no one else was?"

Bob shrugged his shoulders. "That's what he said, yes."

"That's what the DVD would have shown me?" Silas asked as he finally began to eat his scrambled eggs.

"Yep. He went deep into it, naming names and everything. I started to stop the camera, but my wife told me to let it roll. He was being so real. We didn't make that DVD available to the congregation. My wife has always worried people would think it was us, so she suggested we keep this DVD just in case."

"So why would someone steal something like that if they know you could just tell me."

"Well, they had no idea you had that copy. At least I don't know how they would. So they were coming after you for some other reason and took the DVD just in case, probably."

That's the same thing Silas had already thought. He usually tried not to trust anyone when he worked a case, but his instincts were telling him he could trust this man.

"So is this tent revival still going on? If they're halfway across the country, I can probably rule them out as the people who are messing around in this. It doesn't clear them for the murder, but it lets me know they aren't the ones who came to my home."

"They opened a church here in town several months ago. Bodean's wife is from here. That's how they knew Tucker in the first place."

"What's the name of their church? Silas asked quickly.

"Abba's Prayer and Revival House."

"Like that band that sings Dancing Queen? My daughter used to play them all the time. I pretended not to like them, but they had some catchy tunes."

"You didn't grow up in church, I take it," Bob said.

"I was Presbyterian," Silas said. "I guess it didn't fully stick."

"Well in some churches, they call God, Abba. It's like calling him Daddy."

"Who calls God, Daddy?" Silas asked. He finished his coffee and reached for the pot the waitress had left on the table. "Isn't that disrespectful?"

"I don't know. I just think it's strange," Bob said. "I don't do it. And Bodean, now that he's off the road and building up this big church, has the congregation call him Daddy Bo."

"Daddy Bo?" Silas asked as he slowly shook his head.

"Can you tell me where to find this church?" Silas asked.

"Do you know where the old Rose's Department Store used to be?" Bob asked as he finished his last piece of bacon.

"I think so. Remember, I haven't always lived here. Is it over in that old strip mall next to the airport?"

"That's the one. He built his church right in the middle of that strip mall. You can't miss it. You may wish you had, but trust me. You can't miss it."

Chapter 5

Churches were not supposed to look like this one did. That was just Silas' opinion of course, but he didn't like how big it was and how damn tacky it was. He remembered attending a little Presbyterian church in St. Louis when he was young, and a bigger but still small church of the same type when he was a bit older. In his mind, churches were meant to represent humility and usually reflected scarcity or even poverty. Wren River Baptist was a modest and humble looking building. That was how he always pictured Jesus-simple, modest, and humble.

That did not appear to be how this church pictured Jesus. As he neared what he assumed was the main entrance, a thirty foot tall statue of a long haired man in flowing robes towered over him with one arm swept outward and the other arm extended forward with a thumbs up. This Jesus had a big smile on his bearded face, and he was winking.

The main entrance doors were locked. It was a Wednesday and not a Sunday, so Silas had to remind himself not to be surprised that the church was closed. As he made his way around the building he tried each door but those were locked as well. The parking lot had several cars in it, but they could have belonged to people shopping at the other stores in the strip mall. There was a Best Buy and a Party City on either side of the church.

Silas doubled back around to the main entrance so he could try to see through the glass doors. The glare from the sun had made them seem mirrored. After cupping his hands and leaning close, he discovered that they didn't just appear to be mirrored, that's exactly what they were. Each door was an eight foot tall, three feet wide mirror with different questions stenciled on the top portion. One asked, "Who is your worst enemy?" The door next to it asked, "When did you last tell this person you love them?" Silas watched himself smile in the mirror and shake his head.

A clicking sound to his left caused Silas to jump. One of the mirrored doors opened and a man with a thick southern accent said, "Can I help you brother?" To Silas, it sounded like, "Ken ah hep yewwww brawthur?"

"I hope so," Silas said. "I'd like to speak with Bodean Culp if I could."

"He's expecting you?" the man asked. He had one boot holding the door open, and the other extended outward, while the bulk of his big body leaned on the door frame. He was wearing all black. The t-shirt said, "Abba's House". There was a name tag on the man's chest, but Silas couldn't read it.

"No," Silas said. "I guess I need to make an appointment. Unless he's around?"

"Come on in," the man said. "My name's Richard." As Silas walked past him through the door, he read the nametag. It said, "Big Dickie".

If Silas had thought the outside of the church didn't look like a church, the lobby didn't serve to change that opinion at all. There was a giant fountain in the center of the lobby and the lights made the water appear to be red. A sign in front of the fountain said, "J.C.'s Wishing Well". Music blared from unseen speakers. Large screens with various scenes and images were scattered across the walls. One advertised a trip to Haiti. The one next to it invited guests to something called a spontaneous baptism.

Richard led Silas to a solid looking door on the far side of the lobby and opened it to reveal an office with at least four women working from cubicles. One of the women looked up and exchanged a look with Richard before standing and walking over to Silas. "May I help you?" she asked.

"He wants to make an appointment to see Daddy."

"Reverend Culp?" she corrected. Then she turned to Silas. "You want to make an appointment to see Reverend Culp?

"Oh yes ma'am," Silas said. And then he added, "Please."

"What is the purpose of your visit?" she asked.

"Well," Silas said. "I wanna join the church."

"Oh that is wonderful," she said. "But normally anyone who wants to join the church would sign up for our new members class, which is taught by Reverend Culp on Wednesday nights."

"That's tonight," Silas said with a smile.

"Yes it is," she said, returning the smile.

"Well where do I sign up for this class? I'm in!" he said with as much false enthusiasm as he could muster.

"I can send a link to your phone if you'd like," she said.

Silas smiled again, this time genuinely. "Well thank you for that, but I don't think that would help me very much."

"Well, then you could always just drop by this evening and I will get you in the class," she said with a big smile. She touched his arm and said, "We wouldn't ever turn away a lost sheep." She looked around the room quickly and lowered her voice. "Or are you a black sheep?"

"I would say I'm a bit of both," Silas said, reminding himself to smile and make eye contact.

"See you tonight...What's your name again?"

"Steven Burch," he said without hesitation.

"My name is Viola. See you tonight, Steven," she said, running her hand down his arm to his wrist before letting go.

"You know you will Viola," Silas said as he walked out the door. Richard was waiting for him in the lobby and walked him out the front door. "Have a good day, sir," he said, as Silas made his way down the sidewalk and out of the shadow of the thirty foot Jesus. Silas raised a hand up over his head, made a backwards wave, and continued towards his truck, which he had purposefully parked far enough away to make his license plates almost impossible to see.

With both windows down in his truck, the wind blowing across his face felt good. Not only was it keeping him awake, it was clearing his mind. The blow to his head had put him in a bit of a fog, but the fog seemed to have lifted. He would return back to the church later in the day, but for now, he needed to figure out his money situation. If he didn't find Larry, he was working this case for free, and it didn't take away from the fact that he needed cash in the next few days, or he was going to start losing things. He needed two grand by Friday, or the electricity would be cut off at the trailer park. If his tenants lost power, this gave them an excuse, and a damn valid one in his mind, to leave without paying their rent. Several of the tenants owed him past due rent, and they were the reason he couldn't pay the electric bill, but the minute the power went out, they would start packing, and he would never see another dime from any of them. Beyond that, many of the residents of the park were families, and the last thing he wanted was for them to lose their power and eventually lose their home. He had a responsibility to them as the landlord (he hated that term) and to not keep that responsibility made him sick to even think about.

He also owed personal property taxes in a week. If he didn't pay those, since he was already past due, a Deputy Sheriff would appear at some point with a summons. That summons would cost him his private investigator's license. The state of Kansas was stingy with their issuing of licenses, and they seemed to always be looking for a reason to take one back.

His mind kept shifting back and forth between the case, and his money situation. He was trying to keep his thoughts busy so that he didn't think about Pete. It didn't work, though, so as he drove, he reached for his wallet, opened it up while steering the truck, and pulled out the I.D. from the wallet Tommy found. The address was in a shitty part of town, less than ten miles from the trailer park.

When he arrived there, the building didn't look like a place where people lived. It was a pawn shop. As Silas read the sign above the door, a smile made an uninvited but not unappreciated visit to his face. Vickerson Pawn and Loan. The name on the I.D. was James Vickerson, Jr. Two quick right turns brought Silas onto a street that ran along the back of the building. In a side lot, he spotted the Subaru Outback Tommy told him about. After parking behind the Outback, blocking it in, Silas jumped out quickly. As he closed the truck door, he looked at the shotgun and decided against it. He also chose to leave the pistol. Instead, he pulled an axe handle and a pipe wrench from the toolbox on the back of his truck.

The address was #4. There were no numbers on the doors, but there were letters. He gambled that room D was #4, and as his work boot kicked hard against the doorknob, he hoped he had chosen correctly. The face of the man on the couch matched the picture on the I.D. Even in the surprised state he was suddenly in, it was no question this was the same man. Another man came out of a side room and yelled, "What the hell, Jimmy?"

A blood soaked bandage on the man's left arm told Silas everything he needed to know in order to let the axe handle swing. The first blow landed on the side of the tall man's right knee. On the backswing, he caught the man's already wounded left arm. The handle landed squarely against the elbow and the man's screaming didn't even drown out the sound of bone cracking. With the one man now out of the fight, Silas threw the pipe wrench like a tomahawk and it landed square against Jimmy's chest, causing the little man to make a face like he needed to cough and throw up at the same time. When he recognized Silas, Jimmy did both. The cough was first, followed by a gagging sound and a mess all over the thick brown rug and matching paneling on the wall.

Silas retrieved the pipe wrench, which had bounced off of Jimmy's chest and landed on the cluttered coffee table. He looked between Jimmy and the other man, and decided that Jimmy was occupied for at least a few minutes, freeing him up to pay some more attention to the tall man, who was now down on one arm and one knee. The other arm and knee were out of commission. Silas dropped to one knee, looked back over his shoulder to make sure Jimmy wasn't going to insert himself into the conversation, and lifted the man's face up so they were looking directly at each other. "Do you recognize me?" Silas asked.

The man nodded quickly, which briefly gave him the appearance of a bobble head doll.

"That's good," Silas said. "I was worried you wouldn't, since judging by the wounds to your arm, you were the one hiding under my deck like a little bitch pervert hoping to peep up under some skirts.

The man grunted and tried to raise himself up enough to lunge at Silas. The lunge ended up looking like a pathetic wriggle.

Silas shook his head and laid the pipe wrench across the fingers of the man's right hand. "I weigh about 190 pounds," Silas said. "Now, since I'm tall, I come across looking lean. Some might say skinny, but I know I'm not that. Not since Junior High School and that was a long time ago. I am lean though, and it makes my nearly 200 pounds look light. But when I stand on that wrench and bounce a little… Damn, son, your fingers are gonna snap like stale bar pretzels."

The man made a whimpering sound and Silas knew it was question and answer time. "Who sent you to my house?"

"I don't know," the man said through clenched teeth.

"Who sent you to my house?" Silas asked again, as he stood up and moved his boot onto the wrench.

"I don't know," the man said again. He was whimpering now.

Silas put a bit of his weight on the wrench and the man began to shout, "His dad told us to!" He pointed at Jimmy with his one good hand. "Jimmy's dad paid us to do it!"

Silas moved his foot off of the wrench and looked quickly around the room. "Get up and move over to this closet," Silas said as he opened the little door and pulled the vacuum cleaner out. "Get up and get in here now," he said, raising his voice.

The man moved towards the closet slowly and fell twice on his way across the small room. After he was finally in the closet, Silas said quietly. "Did you kill my dog?" The man didn't respond, but instead, he started crying quietly. "You did?" Silas asked. The man nodded. "I hope he haunts your dreams, you son of a bitch," Silas said as he shoved his boot against the man's forehead, sending him thudding limply against the back closet wall.

Jimmy had almost made it to the front door when Silas caught his ankle with the axe handle. The short man landed backwards onto a coat rack which served to hold him in a standing position for at least ten seconds before the rack snapped in half, allowing Jimmy to continue his trajectory to the floor. Silas was over him before he even fully landed. "Why did your daddy send you to my trailer park?" Silas asked.

Jimmy tried to crawl towards the couch.

"The more times I ask, the more fingers I break," Silas said.

Jimmy crawled faster towards the couch and lunged forward, his hand sliding up under the couch, reaching for what Silas could only assume was a gun-maybe a knife, but most likely, a gun. Grabbing Jimmy by the ankle, Jimmy dragged him back away from the couch and dropped a knee hard onto his spine. He felt something give, which caused Jimmy to scream in agony. Now Silas had found the spot to work. He moved his knee forward, feeling the popping in

Jimmy's back again. As Jimmy was catching his breath and seemingly preparing to scream again, Silas leaned forward and asked, "Why did your daddy send you to my trailer park?" He pushed down on the spine again and Jimmy screamed.

"Something to do with his church. He said you were hurting his church." After he said it the boy (and that's what he really was, though he was probably in his early twenties) began to sob.

"What church?" Silas asked as he grabbed the boy's earring and began to twist it.

This caused the boy to scream even louder, and when, to Silas' own shock, the earring broke off, taking Jimmy's earlobe with it, Silas instinctively dropped it, causing Jimmy to see it. When he realized what it was, Jimmy let out a silent scream and then passed out.

"Dammit!" Silas yelled. Such a stupid thing to do, causing the boy to pass out before he could tell him what he needed to know.

"Which church?" he said to himself as he drove his truck through back streets, avoiding the sirens that would be inevitable. First, the paramedics. Next the police. He cursed himself again for not giving that stupid boy the time to confess. Now we was stuck with the same question that had been swirling around underneath the surface of the waters in this case. Which church had something to do with the murder of Tucker Robertson? Was it Wren River? The church he left his estate to had motive. But so did Bodean Culp and his church. Tucker Robertson had already shared at least part of his story with the

Wren River congregation. How long before the old man, in his newly found repentant state, had told someone there everything about the con-man who was setting up shop right down the road?

One of the churches wanted to stop his investigation so badly that they had sent out thugs to discourage them. The father who sent the boy and his friend had either overestimated what the two boys could do, or he had underestimated what Silas could do. Either way, Jimmy Vickerson Sr. was trying to protect his church by intimidating Silas. The obvious way to figure that out was to stake out the pawn shop and follow Vickerson to church. The police would be everywhere for the rest of the day, so he would have to be careful hanging around what was now a crime scene.

Chapter 6

The church looked different somehow with people all around. And people were everywhere. The main lobby was packed. Men and women were either in line for a coffee drink, or standing around drinking one. Everyone was talking and the sound they generated was like a flock of turkeys in a small room. Kids were everywhere as well. They even seemed like they were drinking coffee, or they were running around like they had been drinking some. Kids and adults alike were pitching coins in the wishing well, or prayer fountain, or whatever it was called. Over in one corner of the big welcome area, a man was playing a folk guitar and a small group of people were singing along with a song Silas didn't recognize.

Silas made his way through the crowd to the door that he had gone through earlier that day. So much had happened, it seemed like he had visited the church a week ago, but it had only been hours. As he walked through the door, the office atmosphere from earlier had been replaced by what had more of the appearance of a family meeting. One man was talking and the others, mostly ladies, were sitting around listening and giving feedback.

When the man at the front of the room spotted Silas, he stopped talking and asked, "May I help you, brother?"

"Oh I'm just here to see Viola," Silas said awkwardly. His eyes were searching for her but he didn't find her.

From behind him he heard a woman's voice say, "Steven is with me, Drew. He's my guest." It was Viola. She was wearing a summer dress, her hair was down, and she looked twenty years younger.

Silas smiled when he saw her. And it was a genuine smile which surprised him. He had been under the recent impression that he had run out of genuine smiles for people.

In as unison as a dozen people could be, the other people in the room said, "Welcome Steven!"

Viola smiled and clapped, letting out a squeal of approval. Silas waved back at everyone and then turned to Viola. "I'm ready for that new people's class. Or visitor's class," he laughed. "Whatever it's called, I wanna go."

"Well, follow me, cowboy," she said with another squeal.

As they walked out of that room, Drew started talking again behind them as the door shut, and they emerged back into the crowded lobby, which was becoming less crowded by the second as groups of people and singles dispersed through different doors around the lobby. "Service is starting," she said.

"Is that where we're going?" Silas asked.

"No," Viola said. "I thought you've been here before."

"I have," Silas lied.

"Well, then as you know, Reverend Culp preaches in here, and the membership class is just down this hallway here," she said, as she led the way.

"I thought Reverend Culp taught this class," Silas said.

"He does," she said, smiling. "He teaches every class in the building. By recorded video."

"Oh," Silas said. "Well, hey, how about we go to the big service?"

Viola moved her head slowly to the side like she was trying to stretch her neck. "Why?" she asked. "I thought you wanted to join."

"Well," Silas was trying to think quickly. "I was just thinking we could sit in there on some comfortable seats and learn together, instead of in some classroom sitting in folding chairs."

Viola fought a smile, but only for a second before letting it spread across her face. "Well I have jobs to do so I might have to keep getting up and taking care of stuff. I have responsibilities."

"Oh I understand," Silas said. "I would never try to get in the way of a working woman. But maybe you could sit with me as much as possible?" he asked, this time using a full on grin instead of the thin smile.

"That sounds like a plan I can get behind," she said, as she led him back across the lobby and through the doors leading into what she called, the main sanctuary.

As they walked through the doors, the first thing Silas thought was that he was entering a rock concert. Different colored lights and spotlights. Loud music. Fog machines. Strobes. He had gone to a Bon

Jovi concert back in the 90's and this looked even fancier than that show.

As Viola led him up steps that led to stadium style seating, Silas almost felt dizzy being so high up with all the lights and smoke. She pointed him to a row of empty seats and then leaned in and said, "Get comfortable. I'll be back."

Silas smiled and gave her a small wave before she turned around and descended the stairs and disappeared in the dim and purple lighting.

Silas could not get over how big the main sanctuary was. It looked like twenty of the Wren River Baptist Church buildings could fit in there. The stage alone was bigger than his trailer. The drum set was massive and took up the back quarter of the stage as two drummers banged out their rhythms on skins and cymbals. In front of them, a man in a shiny shirt sang to God while men and women danced and played other instruments. A choir swayed with the rhythm and sang loud and in as close to one voice as forty plus people can. They weren't wearing robes, but they all wore the same color yellow t-shirt and black pants. A second smaller choir moved throughout the sanctuary like a singing flock of geese flapping their arms and getting the people to rise up. They were wearing white t-shirts and jeans.

Suddenly, the man in the shiny shirt stopped singing, but the music kept playing and even got louder as he started to shout like the man at the boxing matches who introduces the next fighters.

"Awwwww give it up, give it up, give it up for our Pastor. The founder of Abba's Prayer and

Revival House! Our friend, our brother, our DADDDDDDY, Bodeeeeeeeeeeeean Cullllp!

As Bodean Culp took the stage, the praise continued on in a life of its own, like a cyclone that touches down on a busy street. He gladly stepped into it and let the energy swirl all around him. Bodean did not look the way Silas expected. Based on everything he had seen already, he expected some over the top outfit, but that wasn't the case. Bodean was dressed in a white shirt with a brown suit jacket, dark blue jeans, and cowboy boots. No tie. His hair was short and bright white.

"Do you know how much I love you?" Bodean Culp asked into the microphone?

The crowd yelled "Yes!"

He smiled a big smile and asked louder, "DO you know how much I love you????!!!!"

"YESSSS!" This time applause and shouts were mixed in.

"I WISH it was possible for you to REALLY KNOW how much I love you!" he shouted.

Silas watched as the crowd continued to do things like the crowd at a rock concert. They shouted Bodean's name in different forms ranging from "BO DEAN" to "DADDY DEAN" to "CULP CULP CULP". The shouts went throughout the room in waves. Sometimes the waves collided, and sometimes they combined to form one big wave of energy that made the room seem like outer space.

When they got ready to pass the offering plate, a woman took the stage and talked about how the church had helped her when she was homeless.

Another man came forward and said the church paid for his electricity. An older man spoke about how they fed hungry people every week. And then the plate was passed while the man in the shiny shirt sang another song Silas didn't recognize. They called this part of the show, the offering, and it seemed to Silas like this was the part that everyone's performance so far was pointing towards. The plates that were passing all around him were filled with envelopes and checks and cash. There was also a giant screen that played a looping video that showed how people could give by using their phone or tablet. Silas could not believe the amount of money circulating through that room. He reminded himself that Sunday morning had to be way bigger than this since that was the traditional time people went to church. That would make this the side offering. If this was the gravy on the biscuits, what the hell did the biscuits look like?

An older man came on the stage next to Bodean and prayed a blessing over what he called "the message" and at another time in the prayer he called it "the sermon" and at another place he called it "a word from God".

When Bodean began to speak, Viola came up and sat in the seat next to Silas. The lights dimmed when the sermon started, like the movie theaters do when the movie is about to begin. Silas felt Viola's arm touch his and then he felt their legs touch. Lightly. Not enough to be inappropriate necessarily, but for Silas, anything like that was inappropriate in church, no matter how old you are. He reckoned, in his mind, that even married couples shouldn't touch in church. That did not appear to be how Viola saw it. Her hand on his knee told him she had a much different definition of appropriate.

Bodean Culp did not shout or dance around during the sermon the way he did when he was introduced or during the offering. Instead, he stayed soft spoken. He seemed more like a storyteller. And that's exactly what he was doing-telling a story. This one was about the time when he was just a kid when the town drunk got hit by a car and was taken to a hospital a few hours away where he laid in a hospital bed in a coma. Silas was having a bit of a hard time following along, because at the same time Viola's hand began to rhythmically squeeze his knee, he also started to realize just how tired he was. He had been up since very early, and any sleep he had gotten before that was because he had been whollopped in the head from behind. He wasn't sure if unconscious and sleep were the same thing, but he suspected their impact on the human body was at least somewhat different. Regardless, he was tired, and as Bodean talked about the fact that everyone in his town thought the old man was dead, because in those days there was no internet or cell phones and limited forms of communication caused everyone to be ignorant to the fact that the town drunk was in a coma, and not dead, Silas had to admit, he was totally clueless as to what the preacher was trying to preach about.

Something happened about thirty minutes into the message, though. Just as Viola was increasing the pressure of her squeeze, and Silas was fighting to keep his eyes open, Reverend Bodean Culp's volume increased dramatically.

"BUT ONE DAY, FRIENDS, CHILDREN, BROTHERS, SISTERS, ONE DAY, OLD LEROY GAINES CAME WALKIN' INTO TOWN. AND I WANT YOU TO KNOW HE WASN'T STUMBLING LIKE HE USED TO. HE WASN'T DRAGGIN' ALONG LIKE HE USED TO. HE WASN'T SWERVING ALL OVER THE PLACE LIKE HE USED TO. NO NO. NO NO. HE HAD A LITTLE BIT OF A STRUT TO HIM" At this point in the message, Bodean began to strut across the stage. "AND PEOPLE ALL SAID THE SAME THING WHEN THEY SAW LEROY. THEY SAID 'WE THOUGHT THAT OLD MAN WAS DEAD'. AND YOU KNOW WHAT? THEY WERE RIGHT. BECAUSE AT SOME POINT IN THAT COMA, LEROY GAINES WAS VISITED BY THE PHYSICIAN OF ALL PHYSICIANS. THE DOCTOR OF ALL DOCTORS. THE SURGEON OF ALL SURGEONS. THE KING OF KINGS. AND THAT OLD MAN IN THE BED? THAT OLD TOWN DRUNK? HE DIED. AND A NEW MAN GOT UP OUT OF THAT BED AND STRUTTED ON HOME. YOU SHOULD HAVE SEEN IT. IT WAS A SCENE TO BE SCENE MY FRIENDS. HE WAS STRUTTING AND DANCING AND INTRODUCING EVERYONE TO THE NEW LEROY GAINES!" Bodean began to strut and dance and hop all over the stage at that point, periodically stopping to wave at the crowd or to signal for them to shout louder.

If Silas thought the crowd had gone crazy before, what they were now was pure insanity. "I want you to repeat after me," Bodean said into the microphone. "The old man is dead. Say it with me. The old man is dead. Come on down to the altar if you have ever treated a dead man like he was the same man. Come on down if you need to die tonight and be re-born. Come on down and get freed from that. Come on. Come on."

Viola was on her feet and halfway down the steps before she ran back up to tell Silas she would see him after the service. She made it halfway down again before she ran back up and asked, "Do you wanna come down with me?"

"I'm fine, but thank you," Silas shouted to be heard over the music.

She smiled and gave him a thumbs up and then ran back down the steps again before she disappeared in the crowd of people making their way to the altar.

"Friends? Brothers? Children?" Bodean called out from the front. "While we spend some time in prayer, for anyone staying in their seats, I ask that you pray for our business owners who sponsor this mid-week service. We put all of their names right up there on the big screen. Y'all pray for 'em now," he said.

Silas began to look all around the sanctuary hoping he would see something that would help him solve the case or even move it ahead a step. Over the years he had come to realize that the breaks in the case rarely came in the form of a smoking gun or a confession letter. Usually it was something smaller. Or several small things that added up.

As his eyes moved from the rows of people to the altar to the screen, he couldn't help but smile, because while the breaks in a case usually come in the form of small hints and clues and pieces of the puzzle, sometimes there is a smoking gun. And sometimes, that smoking gun is right in front of you. The screen that made Silas smile when he read it was sandwiched between an ad for a plumbing company and a Real Estate Broker, was Vickerson Pawn and Loan.

Silas stood up slowly and looked around for Exit signs. He spotted two. One was closer, but crowded with people. The other was a bit further away, but not many people were near it. He chose that one and made his way to it and through it as quickly as he could.

That exit led him into a back hallway where families were coming out of a smaller room at the back of the building. As Silas followed them to a big set of double doors that led outside, a smiling woman who was handing out what appeared to be flyers, handed him one and said, "See you Sunday at 11, we hope." She then looked to the person behind Silas and repeated, "See you Sunday at 11, we hope."

Silas folded the flyer and shoved it into his back pocket.

By the time he pulled into his favorite hot dog stand, he realized he hadn't eaten all day. He ordered three chili dogs and a large order of fries. As he ate, he did some thinking. It seemed like all signs were pointing to Bodean Culp as the killer. Why would an innocent man send thugs to his house just after he was hired to investigate the murder? He had motive. Tucker was starting to talk about his life as a con man, and at the center of that life was Bodean Culp.

Silas finished his second chili dog and started in on the fries. If Culp was his main suspect, was it time to get the police involved? Usually, he would say yes. But based on how Sergeant Mesa had treated him just for checking in on the case, Silas figured he'd better gather some more evidence first.

After he finished his food, he decided to head on back to his trailer. Reminding himself what had happened the last time he walked into his home, Silas drove through the lot looking for unfamiliar cars before parking so close to his trailer that he had to squeeze through his truck door. He grabbed the shotgun and entered the trailer slowly, checking behind every door and making sure any hiding place was clear. Once he felt like the trailer was empty, he began to secure the trailer by stacking two towers of soup cans against each door. He needed to make sure no one was breaking in while he slept. If they did, Silas made sure they would make enough noise to wake him up and receive a greeting they wouldn't want to get. He had once been in a similar situation and had thought he solved the problem by stacking heavy furniture in front of the doors. Halfway through the night he realized he had actually trapped himself inside the house just as much as he had blocked other people out. The soup cans were a better compromise to the heavy furniture.

Chapter 7

Silas was awake and positioned behind his desk with the shotgun braced across it and aimed at the door by the second set of knocks on the front door. After a long stretch of silence a voice called out, "Mr. Buchanan? It's me. Larry Robertson." Silas moved out from behind the desk, down the hall and then, after navigating around the tower of soup cans, he slipped quickly out the back door and jumped over the railing and off of the deck. As soon as he landed on his feet, Silas swung the big shotgun around, making sure no one was out there in the dark. When he rounded the corners to the front of the trailer, he could clearly see Larry, alone on his porch.

"I'm gonna need you to show me your hands, Larry."

The man jumped backwards so quickly from fright that Silas was afraid he would fall off of the porch. He raised his hands way above his head and shouted, "I don't have a gun."

"Come on down off of the porch and get up against the trailer," Silas said.

Larry was silent as Silas moved up on the porch and opened the front door.

Once inside, it didn't take long for Silas to realize the Larry he was talking to now was not the Larry who had come to see him just two days earlier. While he had been nervous and awkward that first time, now he was almost manic. He walked in small circles when he was standing, and he bounced his leg when he was sitting.

"They picked me up, not even ten minutes after I left here," Larry was saying in response to Silas' questions about where he had been. "I stopped for gas, and these guys came up in this car and they threw me in the back of their car while one of them drove mine. I thought I was gonna die."

"Where did they take you?"

"To a building downtown. There were apartments around the back. They took me into #2."

"They let you see where you were going? No blindfold? They didn't make you lie down in the seat?"

"No," Larry said. His leg bounced faster. "And I watched enough of those crime shows growing up. My step dad loved them. And in those shows, man, if the victim saw the bad guy's face-- Or if he knew where he was being held? That meant they weren't planning on him being around long enough to testify or tell anyone what he saw."

"Right," Silas said. He was beginning to feel bad for this guy again. "So what happened? How did you get out?"

"Somebody broke into the apartment above me and beat the ever living hell out of the guys who were up there. I'm assuming they were the same guys who grabbed me. Assholes. I thought they were gonna crash through the ceiling. After that, the rescue squad came. Then another one. Right after that, the police came and started knocking on doors.

They opened the door to the apartment I was in after knocking on it forever, and I shouted out for their help. They untied me, took me to the police station, asked me a bunch of questions, and then let me go."

"They let you go just like that? That doesn't make sense. Even if you were the victim, with what happened upstairs, I would think they would ask you more questions. Did they ask you about me? Or your father?"

"No," Larry said. Suddenly he was more confident. "Well, they started to ask about my father, but I told them I wanted my lawyer there. This one cop, Sergeant Mesa wanted to hold me and he asked questions about my dad, and if I was investigating the case on my own, and if I had hired my own detective, but I said I wanted my lawyer."

"Did anyone follow you here?" Silas asked. "They followed you here a few days ago without you knowing it."

"I don't think so," Larry asked. "Besides, the two guys who followed me are all busted up now."

"I'm not worried about those two guys," Silas said, as he moved to the two lit lamps and cut them off. "I'm worried about Sergeant Mesa." Silas moved from window to window, peering into the darkness, seeing what he could see. This case had suddenly moved forward in giant steps, and he felt like he had trapped himself inside a tin can. "We gotta get out of here," Silas said.

Larry didn't even question him. He just nodded and walked in small circles until Silas went down the back hallway. Larry followed him and walked in circles until Silas emerged from the back room carrying one bulging backpack and a long case. "Hold this," Silas said, handing him the long case while he slung the backpack over his shoulders and drew a revolver from his holster.

Silas led them through the trailer, and into the darkness across the trailer park. When they got to Jenny Mercer's mobile home, Silas stopped Larry and told him to wait in the darkness of the big oak tree on the corner. "Keep that close," Silas said, pointing at the long case.

Larry nodded and backed up as close to the tree as possible.

When Jenny opened the door finally, she was dressed and holding a small pistol.

"Were you expecting me?" Silas asked with a smile as he pointed at the gun in her hand.

"No. One of the girls is having trouble over in my other trailer," she said. "I just tried to call you but you didn't answer. How did you know I needed help?"

"I didn't," Silas said with a short laugh. "I came here because I need your help."

"Well, Siobhan is about to get the shit beat out of her, so can you help me first? Then I'm all yours."

"Deal," Silas said. "I'll be right back."

"Oh I'm going with you," Jenny said quickly.

"Okay," Silas said as he started across the yard towards what Jenny called her "other trailer"." He holstered his pistol again and called out over his shoulder, "Stay where you are, Larry. I'll be right back."

"Who the hell is Larry?" Jenny asked as they walked together into the darkness between her home and her other trailer. As they walked, Jenny filled him in. "Siobhan sent me a message a few minutes ago. Two brothers came in. One paid. The other said he was just gonna wait outside to make sure his brother was safe. They're drunk. The first one got what he paid for, and then he started saying he paid for his brother too. When Siobhan said he didn't, the first brother called the second brother in, and they are refusing to leave until they both leave satisfied. But they refuse to pay any more than they already paid, which was for only one of them."

As they neared the trailer, Silas started to tell Jenny to wait outside, but he knew she wouldn't. It would waste words and time to even bring it up.

Jenny said, "They should be sitting to the right, waiting. Siobhan just wrote me that she told them to wait there while she freshened up." Jenny took a deep breath and pushed the door open as Silas stepped in and quickly turned to his right.

"Okay boys, it's time to go home," he said, almost in a shout, as he grabbed the biggest brother by the collar and dragged him towards the door. "You only paid for one of you. Now both of you have to go," he said as he flung the man across the deck. He gained his footing and started to go back into the house but was stopped by his brother crashing into him and causing them both to land out in the yard. Silas followed the second brother who he had just tossed by grabbing his belt with one hand and his hair with the other.

As they both stood up, Jenny leveled her gun at them and said calmly, "You two assholes made me ask a man for help. Give me the chance to show you just how much that pisses me off." When they didn't move, she raised her voice and fired the gun in the air. "Get the hell out of here and don't think about coming back here again!" she shouted.

At the sound of the gunshot, dogs started barking all across the trailer park.

The younger brother ran to the car first but couldn't open the car door. "It's locked, Brad!" he shouted to his brother. "Unlock it!"

The older brother patted his pockets and then looked around. "I...I must've dropped 'em," he said sheepishly. "Can someone just shine a light out here or something? Damn. I need just a little help"

Silas just shook his head and walked out into the yard, shining his penlight on the ground. "Tell your brother to come on over here and help you."

"Come help me, Boof," the man yelled.

"Your brother's name is Boof?" Silas asked, as he moved his light across the ground in circular motions.

"When he was born, I was only six, and I couldn't say Booth, which was his real name."

"Makes sense," Silas said, as Boof walked up. "Help your brother out, Booth," Silas said.

"How the hell did you lose the damn keys Monte?" Boof asked quickly.

"He knocked me down," the other brother said, pointing at Silas.

"Well, then he should be down on the ground finding the damn keys," Booth said, as he took a few steps backwards.

"You think so?" Silas asked, as he pointed the light at Booth's face.

"I do," Booth said, taking a few more steps back towards the car.

"Well, I don't," Silas said, switching off the light.

"Hey!" Greg said. "Turn that flashlight back on. I can't see a damn thing."

"I was trying to help," Silas said. "By shining my light, I mean. But once your dumbass brother started demanding that I help, it kind of took the generous spirit out of me. So you can look on your own, or you can get your brother to help. I don't give two damns."

"Get on over here and help," Greg yelled at his brother.

"The hell I will," Booth said.

"Why are you so sour all the time?" Greg asked as he crawled around in the grass closer to the trailer.

"You got some tonight. He's about to get some, I'm sure. I'm the only one that didn't," Booth said. "So yeah, I'm sour. Little bit."

"Dammit Boof, I need your help!" Greg yelled. His voice had suddenly become high pitched and it waffled a bit on the last few syllables. "Got 'em!" He jumped up and walked at just slow enough of a pace to show he wasn't scared, but just fast enough to reveal how scared he actually was.

Booth threw up both fingers as they drove away, and Silas just laughed and turned to Jenny. "Once you get Siobhan calmed down and everyone feeling safe, do you mind driving me and that friend of mine out of the park and into town?"

"Of course," Jenny said. "Where am I taking you?"

"To my storage shed," Silas said. "It's time I switched vehicles for a few days."

The Oldsmobile had belonged to his wife. It was her proudest possession until their daughter was born. She used to describe it to people like she was in a car commercial. "It's a 1972 Oldsmobile Cutlass Supreme 442 Tribute. It was available in convertible that year, but I couldn't find it in green and convertible. Daddy found me a white convertible, but I wanted the green and I didn't mind that the roof stayed put. We drove all the way to Tallahassee to pick her up."

The first time she told that story, Silas had thought it odd. She wasn't usually so materialistic and it sounded almost braggadocious, but over time, as they dated, and eventually married, he realized she equated that car with her father, who had died when she was twenty. Just a few years after he bought her that car. Then, when she died, their daughter Ashely had refused to drive it. Seeing the car everyday was like death by a thousand cuts for Silas, so he had parked it in the storage shed, taking it out only now and then to keep it running right and up to date on inspections and tags.

"Where are we going?" Larry asked. He had remained quiet during the ride out of the trailer park and down back road after back road until they reached town.

Jenny had talked during most of the drive over. She seemed at ease with Silas and he with her. Larry wanted to ask Silas if he was in a relationship with Jenny, but he decided against it. Instead, he decided to query about their destination.

"To the quarry," Silas said, matter of factly.

"The quarry where they found my father?" Larry asked.

"Yep," Silas said as he shifted the car into fourth gear and let the engine make the sound his wife had loved so much.

"Why do you need to see where they found him?" Larry asked.

"I don't," Silas responded. "I want to see the ones who did the finding."

Chapter 8

Their names were Danny and Delmar, father and son, in that order. It hadn't taken Silas long to find out who they were and that they had continued to magnet fish at the quarry, even after their big find. Most likely, especially after their big find. They had hit the redneck jackpot when they found that wheelchair, along with Tucker Robertson's remains. A newspaper article with their smiling faces in the picture appeared in the local paper at the top of the fold. The police interviewed them but treated them like heroes, and not criminals. One of the Sergeants even ran out to the Smoke Shak and brought them back barbecue sandwiches. To top it all off, they ended up getting a better fishing magnet donated to them from the local True Value, because their original device was taken into evidence, and the hardware store owner knew they needed their magnet to make a living.

When Silas and Larry parked at the quarry, next to Danny and Delmar's Bronco, the father and son were nowhere to be seen. Silas checked his watch and it was almost midnight. More than likely they had only been there for a few hours, so waiting for them could be an all night affair. Searching for them, around that whole quarry at night, was something Silas decided he simply was not going to do. Silas decided to go with a third option.

"Hey boys!" he yelled as loud as he could. "Danny!?" He paused for a moment and then yelled, "Delmar!?" Silas considered seeing if the shouting did the trick, but instead he figured he would hit his horn a few times for good measure.

"Somebody's here for an ass whippin' Daddy!" a voice called out from down near the water's edge.

"We're not here to get our asses whipped," Silas shouted back. "Or to whip any asses," he quickly clarified.

"What are you here for, then?" another voice asked.

By process of elimination, Silas assumed this was Danny, and the first one was Delmar. "Delmar, I'm Silas Buchanan, and this is Larry Robertson. You found Larry's father out here a few months ago."

"Is he here for the wheelchair?" Danny asked, still in the darkness. "Because we still ain't got that back from the Police yet." His bitterness at this fact was evident.

"No, no," Silas said. "We just wanna ask a question. We're not here to take anything from you or cause you boys any trouble."

"You a cop?" Danny asked.

"Nope," Silas said. "I'm a private investigator."

"You out here to investigate our privates?" Delmar asked. He laughed and then turned to his dad and said, "Did you hear what I asked him? If he was here to investigate our privates."

"That don't even make sense," Danny said. "It sounds like you're hittin' on him. That's sick. Not funny."

"I wasn't hittin' on him. I was warnin' him not to hit on me," a very exasperated Delmar said.

"How? You brought it up," Danny said, as he stepped up into the oval of light created by the Oldsmobile headlights. "Excuse me, gentlemen, my son is a dumbass." He then turned to Larry. "I'm sorry for your loss. My condolences."

"Thank you," Larry said, clearly caught off guard.

"Well," Silas said, deciding to change his tactics and take a big gamble. "I want to make a business proposition to you."

Delmar stepped out of the darkness at that point. "We don't sell sex. See Daddy? I knew he was a pervert."

Silas just looked at Danny who waved a dismissive hand in his son's general direction. "What do you have in mind, Mr. Buckingham?"

"Well," Silas said, trying to think fast and think ahead at the same time, "I want you to keep one big fact in mind before I make my proposal."

"Okay," Danny said, "I can do that." He accented the I part of the statement, which was not lost on Delmar, who grunted his disapproval of the whole conversation.

Silas pulled out his cigarette pack and shook it expertly, causing three filters to protrude for easy retrieval. He offered one first to Danny who accepted, and then to Delmar who at first declined, but then accepted as Silas started to pull the pack back. As they all lit up and smoked for a few minutes, there was silence. And then, Silas said, "That one big fact I mentioned is this. You boys didn't sign some kind of contract or memorandum with the ones that paid you. No affidavit or non-disclosure, or even your basic confidentiality agreement." Silas finished his cigarette and continued. "I mean, that's an assumption on my part at least, but it ain't a giant leap or anything. Since the whole deal was felonious--" Silas looked towards Delmar. "--that means criminal, then it wouldn't make any sense for anyone to sign a legal document. Am I right?"

Danny stared at Silas and then said, "We didn't sign nothin'."

Silas managed to hide his relief, and continued. "And there's no way for them to collect the money back. It's not like they can make a case that you swindled them, or anything. They paid you to lie. You did. That means they got what they paid for."

Danny clearly didn't like the word lie, but Silas pressed on. "So they can't go around claiming they didn't get what they paid for." At this point in the conversation, Silas lowered his voice. "And let's be honest, gentlemen, who are they gonna complain to?"

This seemed to hit home with both father and son as they exchanged looks in the yellow glow of the Oldsmobile headlights. Silas opened up his arms and extended his hands, palms outwards. "That's the fact that I want you to keep in mind. Now here is our proposition. Silas looked quickly towards Larry, who looked like he had to go to the bathroom. "Tell us what really happened. Tell us the story you didn't tell the cops. Tell us what you would have said, before you got paid to switch things up a little."

Danny stared at Silas and then at his boots, then briefly at Delmar. "And what's in it for us?" Danny finally asked.

"My partner here has five hundred dollars for you," Silas said, quickly.

"Oh that ain't shit," Delmar said, no longer content to be quiet. He stepped further into the center of the makeshift circle. Once we tell y'all what you wanna hear, those guys could come back and say we reneged. And you'll be long gone."

"You raise a good point, son." You two will be on your own. But when the hell haven't you been? That won't be anything new." Silas shifted his gaze back to Danny. "Think about it. You can make a bit more money off of this whole thing, plus, you get it off your conscience."

Delmar started to say something, but Danny gave him a look that Silas couldn't see clearly from where he was standing. Whatever the look was, it stopped Delmar from saying anything further.

"We only changed a few things," Danny said. But then he added. "They was big things, though."

Silas stayed quiet, just letting the man speak.

"Like how he was tied to the wheelchair," Danny said quietly. He was being careful not to look at Larry. "They wanted us to say it was just wire. That he was just wired to it by Romex, but that won't true. It was rope. And it was wrapped all around him and tied in the back. They wanted us to say the electrical wire was twisted at the front. So as to show he could do it himself, I suppose."

"You just fucked it all up," Delmar said. "Confessed to a crime, just now. Who's the dumbass? I ask you, Daddy."

Danny ignored Delmar and said, "The other thing was, they told us not to ever tell anyone about the handcuffs we found."

"Handcuffs?" Silas asked quickly. "You found them the same night?"

"Nope," Danny said. "The day before."

"Oh," Silas said, not able to hide his disappointment.

"Don't be sad, friend," Danny said. "Delmar, tell this gentleman what that handcuff was handcuffed to."

Delmar pumped out his frail and emaciated chest before proclaiming, "That handcuff was handcuffed to...a piece of a wheelchair."

"Damn right it was," Danny said, clearly proud of himself. "Part of the wheelchair we pulled out of this here quarry not twenty-four hours later."

Silas held his cigarette out into the night air, letting the orange ember become red in the night wind. "You found a handcuff attached to a piece of the wheelchair that Larry's father was tied to?"

"Yes ma'am," Delmar said, clearly not wanting to be excluded any further from this conversation.

"Don't you wanna know what part it was hooked to?" Danny asked.

"You know I do," Silas said.

"Well, that's gonna cost ya," Danny said.

"Is it something you would tell the police?" Silas asked. "Because that would be worth another five hundred."

"Well, you just proved you don't know shit," Delmar said, with a grin that went from his right ear to his left jawline. "The cops are the ones that told us what not to say." He shook his head, looked at his father, and crooked a thumb towards Silas. "Dumbass."

"You just told him who paid us," Danny said. "That makes you worse than a dumbass."

"What's worse than a dumbass?" Delmar asked, clearly curious.

"A Delmar, that's what," Danny said.

"Thank you for your time, gentlemen," Silas said. He nodded towards Larry, who looked back with a blank expression.

"I'm not paying these guys," Larry said. "They're the reason the damn case got closed. They're liars!"

"Hey you watch what you're calling who," Delmar said. "We're autopreneurs."

"If I pay it, you're walking out of here," Silas said calmly.

Larry looked from Silas to the two men and then up the long road leading out of the quarry. He looked back at Silas and then walked to the car where he turned his back and pulled out his wallet. He turned back around with folded cash and handed it to Danny, who promptly counted it.

"I'll take that other deal you offered. Five hundred more for information about the handcuffs."

"We'll pass on that one," Silas said.

"But you just offered it," Danny said.

"And your son declined it." Silas motioned for Larry to get into the car.

Larry didn't move. Instead, he yelled, "Look out!"

Silas instinctively spun around to face a rushing Delmar who was wielding a large rock above his head. When Silas saw him, he made a sound that had often been effective in stopping attackers who were not yet totally committed to the idea of attacking. The primal yell, as an old cop friend once called it, did its job once again, causing Delmar to freeze just as the rock was going to leave his hands. This sudden change in movement caused the rock to plummet instead of soaring through the air as was originally intended. The plummet ended on both of Delmar's feet, who reacted by letting forth a primal yell of his own.

Larry, who seemed to have a well honed sense of when to promptly exit a confrontational situation, climbed quickly into the Oldsmobile. Apparently the front passenger's seat was a bit too exposed, because he chose to climb into the back seat, where he sprawled out of view.

After Silas backed his way to the car, and then backed up the long narrow road leading away from the quarry and back up to the main highway, he checked on Larry, who was now sitting up in the back seat, and seemed to have calmed down quite a bit.

"What do we do now?" Larry asked. His voice was steady but low.

"We keep on going and solve this case," Silas said.

"But you heard what he said. The police are in on it. They ruled it a suicide and then made sure it would sound like one once those hobos told their story."

"There's more than one police department in the world," Silas said. "In fact, there is more than one in this county.

"The Sheriff's Department?" Larry asked. "Is that where we're going now?"

"Not yet," Silas said. "We can show it was most likely murder, not suicide. But we can't prove who did it, yet. We'll go to the Sheriff when we know who did it, and when we think we can prove it."

"Well, then where are we heading now?" Larry asked.

"First we're going to a friend's bar. He has a loft apartment upstairs. I'm gonna ask him to let us get some sleep there. And then in the morning, we're going to visit your top suspect, to ask advice on how to contact my top suspect," Silas said, as he rolled down his window and lit a cigarette.

As he pulled into the parking lot of Wren River Baptist Church, he looked for the Pastor's car, but he only saw a small minivan parked by the side door. Silas pulled in next to it. Larry was asleep, and since Silas had wanted him to wait outside anyway, he didn't wake him up. The apartment above the bar was nice, but the noise didn't stop until sometime around 3am. Silas didn't sleep much, and he knew Larry didn't either.

"May I help you?" a woman with a large smile said from the doorway after opening it on Silas' third knock.

"I'm hoping I can see Reverend Parks," Silas said.

"I'm the church secretary," she said. "Beverly Riggins."

"Well hello, Beverly," Silas said. And then after an awkward silence, he added. "May I see the Reverend?"

"Of course," Beverly said. "He will be here in about fifteen minutes. Would you like to wait?"

"Sure," Silas said. "Just sit over here?" he asked, pointing to a row of chairs by the door.

"No," Beverly said. "You can wait out here in our sanctuary." She led him through the door and down the short hallway to the sanctuary. She pointed at the rows of pews, and said, "You look like a back row guy, but feel free to sit anywhere you'd like."

As she walked away, Silas thought to himself that Beverly looked like the stereotypical church secretary. In her late forties, maybe early fifties. Graying hair. Forgettable clothing style.

After close to half an hour, Beverly came back in. "He appears to be running late," she said. "I do apologize."

"It's fine," he said. "I didn't have an appointment, so I understand I might have to wait a while."

"You're investigating Tucker Robertson's suicide?" she asked.

"I am," Silas said, seeing no reason not to tell her. "Did you know Tucker?"

"Of course. It's a small church," Beverly said. "And as the secretary, I meet just about everyone. He was a nice old man. Were you hired by the insurance company?"

"No," Silas said. "I work for Tucker's son."

Beverly gave him a strange look. "Oh," she said. And then after a long pause. "I didn't know he had a son." She shrugged her shoulders and walked back towards the door. "I'll let you know as soon as the Pastor arrives," she said as she disappeared into the dimly lit hallway.

Silas said in the silence of the sanctuary and thought about Larry. He viewed this church as the enemy. He had hired Silas to prove that they were responsible for his father's death. The irony, as Silas saw it, was that this seemed to be the only place that really loved Larry's dad. Or at least that's how it seemed.

"Mr. Buchanan," Bob Parks said from the front of the sanctuary as he emerged from a door Silas couldn't see. "You're here to talk about Tuck, I presume?"

"No, sir," Silas said. "Not yet. I stopped by because I have an odd question for you."

"Fire away," he said with a smile.

"I need some ideas on..." Silas tried to think through how to phrase his request. "I need some suggestions as to how to guarantee a pastor would meet with me when I call and ask for an appointment."

"Well," Bob said. "You got me by dropping in and waiting, but that might not work everywhere." It depends on how big the church is and how many pastors they have serving there. You may present an emergency and get a pastor to meet with you quickly, but it might not be the one you want. Or you could ask for the specific Senior Pastor or Lead Pastor or whatever title he goes by, but your appointment might be several days away. Some pastors only meet on Wednesdays and Sundays."

"So, everything is relative to each church?" Silas asked. "Nothing is really consistent from church to church to guarantee a quick meeting?"

"Hmmm," Bob said. "Well. You could always try money."

Chapter 9

"I woke up this morning knowing I was blessed, but I did not know I would be beyond blessed before my second cup of coffee." Culp was talking before he even entered the room. Before sitting down in his white leather chair, he reached over and shook Silas' hand. "When I heard you wanted to meet with me right away, I told Gina to set you up right away. I didn't know until just now you wanted to make a donation."

Silas smiled a big smile, mirroring the face Bodean Culp was making, showing lots of teeth. "Oh that makes me so happy to hear, you have no idea, Reverend Culp. You really don't."

"The people of this community are our heart, but financial donations are our lifeblood." Bodean Culp was bigger up close than he was up on the stage. He was taller than Silas, which put him well over six feet. His shoulders were wide, and his hands looked like turkey breasts. White and round. At one time he was probably athletic. Hints of muscles in his forearms and the way his chest was packed into the bright pink polo shirt he was wearing pointed to a day when he was in shape. Dinner tables had been replaced by drive-thrus for him, more than likely, which had caused flab to cover up any progress he had made in gyms so many years earlier.

"Let me show you where we direct the donations we receive, Mr. Bryant." Culp moved quickly over to a small remote on a table near his office window, and started pressing buttons. A large screen television came to life with images of hungry children being fed around the world. Words scrolled across the screen listing off all of the countries that Abba's House reached the previous year. Scenes of American children playing basketball on inner city basketball courts changed to a Latin American soccer match between kids of neighboring villages which used to battle with spears and rocks, but now settled their differences through sports, according to the words on the bottom of the screen.

By the time the video showed homeless people receiving meals and clothes over the Holidays, Silas felt thoroughly guilty for his charade and he knew he needed to end it, so he began to speak over the video.

Bodean Culp was watching the video even more intently than Silas and he had a massive smile painted across his face. It faded quickly though as the words Silas was speaking began to sink in.

"Like I said, I do apologize. I hate tricking people, but I really did need to speak with you Reverend Culp," Silas was saying. "I was hired by Tucker Robertson's son to investigate his death."

Bodean Culp didn't even fight to keep the smile in place. He saved that for people who deserved it. "You could have just said that, Mr. ummmm is Bryant your real name?"

"No," Silas said. "My name is Silas Buchanan and I'm a private detective and I was hired by--"

"You already said that," Culp said quickly. "The problem is, you have shown you can lie, so I don't know whether anything you say is true or not. That's a hard hump to get over quickly. It took me years to get people to trust me again once I left my past life as a liar and a con man."

"You left that life?" Silas asked.

"I did," Culp said. "And Tucker Robertson left it with me."

"That's not the way I heard it," Silas said.

"Oh yeah?" Culp asked. "Then you're talking to the wrong people."

"You're in the enlightening business Mr. Culp. Could you enlighten me?"

"I could enlighten you about a lot of things, Mr. Buchanan. But I can start with the topic you raised and the reason you are here." When Silas had heard Culp speak from the stage, he had no discernible accent. If pressed, Silas would have said maybe a bit of a California lift to his voice. But here, when he was clearly riled up, a southern accent had made its presence known. "I publicly shut down my tent revivals and stood at the front of several local churches throughout the regions we toured decades ago (he dropped a flat palm onto his desk for emphasis when he said the words 'decades ago') and offered not only apologies, but financial restitution to the communities for the fraudulent claims we had made back then. And did I do that because some court forced me to? No. Did I do it because some law cop was on the outskirts threatening to put cuffs on me? No. I did it because the God I had used for so many years was now using me." His accent was thick now. Silas remembered episodes of Hee Haw he had watched with his Grandpa when he was little. Bodean Culp sounded like the main stars of that show. "And guess what, Mr. Buchanan? Mr. Private Eye? There were two men standing next to me during that apology tour. During the most humiliating time period of my life. Do you want to guess who one of them was? He dropped his palm on the desk again. "Tucker Robertson. The same Tucker Robertson whose death you think I had something to do with."

"I'm not here to pass judgement, Mr. Culp," Silas said. This had gotten away from him quicker than he could stop. "I'm just here to get to the truth."

"That's a load of bull, Mr. Buchanan," Culp said, his volume rising. "If you were out for the truth, you would have done your homework. Who paid for that man's funeral? For his casket? For his cemetery plot? Did you ask those questions? Was it his father? His son? His new church? You bet your ass it wasn't. It was me. If you were here to find out the truth, you would have checked on that kind of stuff."

He pushed an intercom button on his desk and a door opened behind Silas. He turned to see Richard and a man who looked as wide as he was tall come into the room.

"Get the hell out of here, Mr. Buchanan. Good luck on your witch hunt. Do it somewhere else."

"Mr. Culp I--" Silas started to speak, but he felt the men take hold of his shoulders. "That won't be necessary," Silas said, standing quickly and side stepping Richard quickly enough to make it to the door before the big man could touch him again. "I'm sorry this visit didn't go the way I had hoped, Mr. Culp. I apologize."

"It started out with a lie. How else could it have gone?" Culp's volume was lowered and the accent was gone.

Silas tried to close the door behind him, but the short and wide man caught up to him and escorted Silas out through a fire exit where he was left standing alone next to a dumpster.

"Well, that could have gone better," Silas said, as he began the long walk around the building, back to where the Oldmosbile and Larry waited for him.

"How did it go?" Larry asked.

Silas drove out of the parking lot and down the highway a few miles before speaking. "Who paid for your father's funeral?"

"I have no idea," Larry said.

"And for the casket? The cemetery plot?"

"I don't know," Larry said.

"You don't know much, do you?" Silas said. "You don't know a damn thing about your own damn father."

"No," Larry said quickly. "That's why I hired you. You're supposed to find out what I don't know."

"I could spend a year finding out what you don't know, kid," Silas said through gritted teeth.

His anger had built up faster than he was used to and it had boiled over on this kid, fueled by something he couldn't articulate to himself, much less Larry, who he barely knew. Though he didn't like being chastised the way he had been by Culp, that isn't what bothered him the most about the meeting. Over the years, Silas had learned that some people give a certain look when they are guilty and talking about their victim. Not everyone does it, but most do. Silas had never been able to describe it, because it took on a different form in different people, but he could always spot it. Bodean Culp had not given that look when he was speaking about Tucker Robertson. That wasn't enough to clear him of the crime of course, but it was something Silas couldn't ignore. The other thing he couldn't ignore was his instincts, and they were telling him that Bodean Culp wasn't the killer.

"I'm sorry," Silas said to Larry. "I let my temper get away from me."

"It's fine," Larry said. "I think this is more trouble than it's worth. I made a mistake pursuing this thing. It's time for me to go back to Boston."

Silas drove for a few more minutes in silence. He wanted to make an argument against it, but there wasn't much of one to make. "Where can I drop you off?" he asked.

"I've been staying at the Corn Meadow Motel, near the bus station," Larry said. "If you can drop me off there, I'll grab the rest of the money I owe you."

"You don't owe me anything else," Silas said, as he drove towards the Motel. "I didn't solve the case, and I always want my clients to get what they pay for."

Larry didn't respond. Instead, he just turned his head towards his window and stared out into the empty fields.

After dropping Larry off at the hotel, Silas drove back down to the highway and pulled into a Speedy's gas station. He parked at a deserted end of the small parking lot, near a set of dumpsters, and let the waves of disappointment wash over him. He had come up empty on investigations before, of course. And he had let people down before, both as a cop and as a private investigator, but this one was different. He had lost this one because he had relied on too many assumptions during his investigation, and they just didn't pan out.

He had assumed Bodean Culp was guilty because from the minute Silas took the case, he was followed and eventually attacked by two guys connected to Culp's church. He still couldn't be sure why they were following him or why they were at his trailer when he arrived there with the DVD, but Culp wasn't looking like the prime suspect any longer. He had also made an assumption that the folks at Wren River Baptist Church were innocent, though they had the most to gain. That assumption had grown from the other false assumption about the killer being Bodean Culp. His motive, covering up years of fraud, had begun to dissipate, once Culp said he had already publicly confessed to his wrongdoings in years past. Silas would have to confirm that, but his gut told him it was the truth.

He couldn't trust his assumptions, which came from his mind. Could he trust his instincts, which came from his gut?

He had made wrong choices. "Why?" he asked himself. He spoke the question aloud, but didn't need to speak the answer. He had let the need to pay the bills motivate him to push through the case, taking the path of least resistance and not doing the little things that made him a good detective. Silas got out of the car and walked around in a big circle that got smaller as he walked. When he neared the car again after several circles around it, he jumped in, started it, and drove towards The Red Fox Tavern. It was time to pay his bills, and take a break from the Robertson case.

Chapter 10

Jackie Rippshaw was a local artist. Her specialty was dipping knife blades in paint, and stabbing mannequins. She marketed under the moniker, Jackie The Ripper, and she was locally famous. She was also famous on the internet according to her husband, Clint. She had a huge social media following and made more money in a week than Clint's bar made in a month.

Clint had hired Silas to follow her and catch her cheating. Silas had staked out her studio three different times and could never catch her with anyone. He hated this type of work, but it often paid the bills, and a desperate Clint Rippshaw had offered a bonus if he could close the case by Friday. That gave Silas two more days.

Switching away from the Robertson case would allow his brain to rest on those facts and return to them revitalized. The minute he cleared his mind of Larry and Tucker and Wren River and Bodean Culp, he got an idea on how to catch Jackie The Ripper red handed. Or, depending on her artistic choices of paint, green handed, or blue handed.

Silas accelerated onto the highway, on his way to Clint Rippshaw's bar. He crossed his fingers that Clint would be there, and when he pulled into the parking lot and saw his big white Jeep, he knew his luck had turned.

Inside the bar, Silas asked a waitress to get word to Clint that he was there. She directed Silas to a corner table, and Silas took a seat and waited. After a few minutes, the tall, fat Texan plopped down on a chair across from Silas. "What do you know? Did you catch her yet? Tell me you caught her," Clint said.

"Not yet," but I have an idea," Silas said. "I want you to tell me who you think it is."

Clint looked at Silas like he must be joking. "Shit, Silas. If I knew who it was, I wouldn't need to pay you."

"When we were first talking, you spoke in generalities. When I asked specifics, you shied away from answering. I didn't push it then, but I am now. I think you suspect somebody and you couldn't make yourself say it. It's actually normal. We don't want to voice it, because we feel like it makes it more real."

Even in the dimly lit bar, Silas could tell that Clint was getting emotional, so he kept talking. "I think when we met back at my office, you were all fired up and angry, but I didn't really give you a chance to just talk. Stuff like this takes a toll on you. Wears you down."

Clint wiped his eyes quickly and looked around.

Silas lowered his voice to where Clint had to lean towards him. "Fill in the blank for me, Clint. I hope to God it isn't, blank. Say it and fill in the blank. I hope to God it isn't…."

Clint sat for a long moment and finally said, "Gene Harlow. He's my silent partner in this bar.

Old. Fat. Rich. I hope to God it isn't Gene." Clint looked down at his hands as he peeled the label from his beer bottle. "But I think it is. I think it's Gene."

Silas pulled out his pack of Camels and offered one to Clint. Together they smoked in silence, and then Silas said, "I'm gonna need Gene's address, his favorite restaurants, and a fairly recent picture if you have it. Make and model of his car. Stuff like that."

Clint left and came back a few minutes later with an envelope. "If you need anything else, let me know."

Out in the parking lot, Silas opened the envelope and clipped one of the photos to his visor. He read through the notes and drove to Gene's address. No cars were there, but on a hunch, Silas circled the neighborhood and parked down on a corner of the two main streets of the subdivision Gene lived in. He could barely see Gene's house, but no one would arrive or leave without him seeing them. It was almost three o'clock in the afternoon. For people with normal work schedules, this would be an odd time to try to catch them, but according to Clint, Gene owned three bars and a few massage parlors. Jackie was a performance artist who worked odd hours. Three in the afternoon was the equivalent of eight in the morning for people like Clint and Jackie.

After an hour passed, Silas began to question his strategy, but just as he was considering leaving and coming back later, a red BMW drove by. It was Jackie's car. Right behind her was Gene's black Dodge Ram-jacked up with massive tires. It was an obnoxious truck, driven by what Silas was sure was an obnoxious asshole. The BMW pulled up to the house and parked right out front for all the world to see. Gene parked his truck in the garage. They didn't even try to hide her car.

Silas knew that he needed more than a picture of her car right outside. Normally he had all kinds of different ways to get the pictures and proof the client wanted. Following them to a club or a restaurant would almost always produce incriminating pictures. But Clint was paying a bonus for these, and now Silas knew why. He was stuck in two bad partnerships and they were humiliating him. The only person who cheats and doesn't even try to hide their car is someone that doesn't care if they get caught. They probably thought Clint wouldn't do anything about it.

Silas sat for a few minutes. He knew what he needed to do, and though he wouldn't do it for any other client, Clint was different. Back about five years earlier, a girl and a few of her friends came into Clint's bar. The girl had just turned twenty-one. She was celebrating. She left the bar with three men that were well known around that part of town. Her friends didn't even try to stop her. She was so drunk, the men had to carry her out of there. Clint stopped them, and even had to fight them off to get her back into the bar where she was safe. He let her sober up in his office, and then he called her father. Silas would never forget what Clint had done for him that night, and remembering it then, sitting in that truck, just a block away from where Clint's wife was cheating on him, Silas knew it was his chance to pay him back. He grabbed his backpack from behind the seat and grabbed two cameras. One was small and better for quick up close shots. The other one was made for further distances away.

As he got closer to Gene's house, Silas cut through a side yard to approach from the back. And then he caught his break. He heard water splashing on the other side of a high wooden fence. A woman screamed and giggled. A man shouted back and then the sound of someone jumping on a diving board was followed by a shout and a splash.

Through the cracks in the fence, Silas could see enough to know that pictures of what was happening on the other side of those boards would give everything Clint needed to be free of these two leeches. Unfortunately, the cracks in the boards weren't wide enough to take pictures through. The yards all around were too flat. No hills. Silas even had gear in his truck for climbing poles, but there were no poles around to climb. He could probably go get a bucket truck but by the time he got back to take the pictures, surely they would have gone inside. The laughter and splashing continued and then music joined in on the noise.

A man's voice called out "King Stud wants in the barn. You'd better let him in!" A woman squealed in response. Then the music was turned up so loud that even the splashing sounds were drowned out.

Silas walked quickly to the front yard and stopped at the sidewalk before turning around to face the house. The roof could be climbed, but if he was spotted, he would be stuck up there. Getting down would be harder than getting up if he was trying to do it quickly.

To the left was a one story house. Climbing their roof would be possible, but there were kids playing in the front yard. The house to the right of Gene's was a tall craftsman style with patios extending off of each story. The second story patio looked right down on the pool at a perfect angle for what Silas needed to do. He realized he was smiling as he walked to the front door of Gene's neighbor's house, and rang the doorbell. The door swung open quickly, and a man who appeared to be of retirement age stood there for a moment before asking, "Can I help you?"

"Yes sir," Silas said quickly. "Actually, I'm here to see if I can help you. I work for the county, and we just got yet another complaint about this jackass--I mean, your next door neighbor."

"Well my next door neighbor is a jackass," the old man said. "And I've complained about him more times than I can count, but I didn't call this time."

"No sir," Silas said. "Your other neighbor did, I suppose. They called in a public lewdness complaint and a violation of the noise ordinance."

"Oh they did, did they?" the old man said as he stared at Silas. "Well, it's about damn time. What do you need from me?"

"I need to take a video of what they are doing, but the coward hides behind that damn fence. I can't get a good shot."

From behind the man, somewhere in the house, a girl's voice (maybe a teenager) said, "He can use my selfie stick."

"Your what?" the man said as he whirled around to face whoever had spoken from behind him.

"My selfie stick." A young lady who looked to be in her late teens stepped into view. "I use it to take pictures. He could attach it to his phone and hold it up high enough to record everything he needs." She smiled at Silas and he quickly looked away toward Gene's house.

"How many times have I told you to stop with the eavesdropping?" the man said to what Silas presumed was his daughter.

"I just need a minute or two to record what he's doing," Silas said. "And I don't have a phone, so I appreciate your offer. But I just need to use my camera."

"You can use anything you want," she said, as she peeked around her father's shoulders.

"Take your damn selfie stick back in the house, the man said, as he slammed the door on Silas. From within the house he could hear them arguing. For a long moment, he thought the man would come back to the door, but he didn't. Silas walked back to the sidewalk. The music was still playing from Gene's house, but the laughter and voices had stopped. They may have already gone inside. If not, they probably would soon. After walking in a small circle, Silas went back to Gene's neighbor's door and knocked again.

"What the hell?" the man said when he opened the door this time. "I don't want to get involved with whatever this is."

"Here's the truth," Silas said. "Your neighbor's an asshole. And that woman he's with is his business partner's wife. I'm here to get video of it so my client can get out of both of these terrible relationships. Will you help me?"

He hesitated. "I don't know…"

"I'll tell you what," Silas said, thinking fast. "Your daughter looks old enough to date. Am I right?"

"You'd better tread lightly," the man said.

"No, no," Silas said. "I want to make you an offer. I'm a private investigator. If you help me, I'll give you my card. And whenever your daughter dates someone, I'll do a free background check on him. If you let me get a few minutes of video from one of your windows. No questions asked. Anytime you call. I will do a full rundown of any boy who dates your daughter."

The man didn't hesitate. "Well you can see every damn thing from my deck," he said, as he pointed towards the back of his house. "Do you wanna go out there and see what you can see?"

"I sure would," Silas said. "You are a very good citizen, sir. I wish there were more like you in this world. It would be a better place, that's for sure."

Five minutes later, Silas was in his truck with both digital cameras on the seat right next to him, heading back to Clint's bar.

While stopped at a red light, Silas looked to his right at a supermarket parking lot. A lady in an automated wheelchair caught his eye as she made her way out of one of the rooms on the first floor and stopped beside a big Sprinter van. She pushed a button on what looked like a small remote, and a side door opened, allowing a hydraulic ramp to unfold. The van was smaller than Silas thought it would be. It was the size of a normal minivan. His eyes settled on the van for a brief moment as his mind locked in on it as if it were trying to hold onto it as the light turned green and Silas instinctively accelerated. His feet and hands took over and drove the big Oldsmobile down the highway as his mind began to move even faster than the cars around him. For the first time since he had taken the Robertson case, Silas smiled.

Chapter 11

Silas knew he needed to learn the new technology of paying bills using debit cards and computers, but he had stubbornly remained a cash only man while the rest of the world converted to plastic and direct deposit and virtual money transfers. He guessed he was probably the only adult he knew under the age of eighty who had never used an ATM. There was something about holding cash, and going into a local bank to deposit it or withdraw it that he found comfortable. The routine of it was probably the appeal, as he liked to know how and why things worked the way they did, and incorporating all of these new ways of doing things into his daily living was hard for him.

He knew it would be easier to use the new technology, but for now he chose to continue not to. After dropping off the flash drive to Clint, he took the large check the grateful bar owner wrote him and took it to First Community Bank and deposited half of it. The other half he got in cash. The electric bill was too far overdue to pay by check, so Silas drove across town to the only store he knew of that still accepted utility payments. After paying that bill in full, Silas breathed a sigh of relief and sat down at the soda fountain for something he hadn't had in years, a root beer float. As he sat on the old chrome and leather stool, he scribbled in his notepad and began to slowly fit the facts of the Robertson case together like a puzzle. No longer driven to solve the case as quickly as possible in hopes of a fast payoff, Silas could now let his mind work the way it was trained.

On his pad, he wrote names. Several were individuals, but two were churches, and one was a pawn shop. Larry Robertson. Bodean Culp. Quarry boys. Bob ..... Jimmy and .... Jimmy's thug friend. Beverly the church secretary.

His eyes went from name to name, up and down the list and back again. The first question his mind decided to tackle was why James Vickerson had his thugs follow Silas if Culp or Abba's House had nothing to do with Tucker Robertson's death? You don't have to defend the innocent. From the moment Larry had contacted Silas, James had his thugs sniffing around. Silas wrote the names of James and his son and friend and then drew a big question mark next to them.

Why did the police want the murder to be considered a suicide?

Who was missing from this list?

The man who had brought him the root beer float came back around and asked if he would like anything else. Silas didn't answer. He was stirring the remains of his drink and staring at his notepad. Who was he missing from his list?

He stared at the notepad and added "Pastor Bob's Wife" to the list. On a separate page, he wrote down the other question in his mind. "Why did the police want the murder to be considered a suicide?" He stared at that question and then scribbled down another one. "Why did Pawn Shop go to such great links to stop Silas' investigation?"

Silas looked back at the list of names and read each one. Shuffling back to the page with the questions, he wrote a third one: "Why didn't the grandfather leave Larry any money?" Next, he added: "Is the grandfather angry with Larry?" He read that one again, and quickly added, "Is the grandfather angry with the church?"

Back on his list of names he wrote: "The third man?" This was both a person and a question, so he shifted back to the other page and wrote: "Who was the third man with Culp and Robertson when they apologized for being frauds?"

At the top of the page, in a space he had left open, he wrote: "Who is my number one suspect?" Next to it, he wrote a name. "Beverly". Next to that name he wrote "Bob". He didn't want to write Bob's name down, and his gut still said he was innocent, but if Beverly was guilty, wouldn't Bob have to be?

Though he had started out as a patrol officer, he had spent most of his time as a cop, sitting at a desk. For a time, he just processed warrants and evidence tags and finished reports for the patrol officers who didn't have enough hours in their shift to complete them on their own. Eventually, though, he began to help some of the detectives, though he wasn't considered much more than a secretary. He was angry all the time back then. Angry and bitter. So he funneled that energy into solving crimes from his desk. Asking questions. Thinking up more questions. Making lists of suspects. Crossing one off at a time. Eventually, he became one of the lead investigators. His job was to focus on the file, and try to solve the case from the paperwork. More times than not, he did.

That was how he had spent most of his law enforcement career, and he had planned on continuing that style when he became a private investigator. For a while, he had approached each case systematically and intellectually, but eventually, the pressure of managing a mobile home park, and keeping the lights on and the water running and the mortgage paid and the taxes up to date began to change how he did everything, including his detective work.

As he looked from one page to another, he felt his mind come alive. Going from name to name, he asked himself if there was anyone he could rule out. Danny and Delmar were guilty but most likely not for the murder of someone they found the body of. He wanted to think Bodean Culp was guilty of the murder, but he just didn't think he was. Silas started to mark a line through Bodean's name, but he hesitated and put a question mark after his name instead. Sergeant Mesa was probably not the killer, but he was covering it up. Why?

He read through each name again, this time looking for someone other than Danny and Delmar he could remove from the list. When he reached the names of the father and son and thugs, he wondered if they were the killers, and Bodean Culp had ordered them to do it. They had killed Pete. Could they kill a human? Over the years, Silas had found that anyone who can hurt a dog is fully capable of hurting a person. What was their purpose-these thugs? Why did they care? Silas looked around the pharmacy and laughed as his eyes locked in on a Trojan display. "They were protection," he said out loud. "They thought they were protecting him." He quickly wrote on his question sheet, "Their actions don't mean Bodean was guilty. It just meant they thought he was, and they wanted to protect their pastor." Did that mean Culp had to know about it? Not necessarily.

Silas sat up straight on the bar stool and quickly moved the list back on top. His number one suspect was Beverly. Her motivation could be that she thought she was protecting her pastor or her church. And just like Culp with his thugs, Bob didn't necessarily have to know Beverly did it.

But if she did do it, how could he prove it?

Chapter 12

"Willie's Weiner Stand," Delmar said. "Off of Route 40. By the landfill."

"Hell no," Danny said. "Monroe's Kitchen. Past the bus yard."

"Well," Silas said, as he downshifted the Oldsmobile and let the car work its way through the series of curves in the road leading away from the quarry. "Y'all are gonna have to pick one. Taking you to both of those places ain't part of the deal."

"Well, we want to renavigate the deal. You have to take me to Willie's Weiners and you ALSO have to take Daddy to Monroe's."

"And don't forget the hundo," Danny said as he stared out the car window.

"What?" Delmar asked quickly. "He's giving you a hundred dollars?"

"I misspoke. I meant to say hotdog," Danny tried to explain.

"Bull baloney," Delmar said from the backseat. Surprisingly, he didn't say anything more for several miles. When they reached the gravel road, the silence, combined with the random popping of the gravel against the underside of the car or the hubcaps apparently became too much for him and he spoke again. "If I do this, I want more than the meal, too. I want my hundo."

"In all actuality, I only need one of you, and I prefer your father, so whatever you get is more than you should get, because you aren't gonna earn it," Silas said. He didn't like Delmar. He found himself liking Danny, which really didn't surprise him. He had hoped to like Delmar, because he usually liked most people, but Delmar was like a urinal where someone puts a garbage bag over it and tapes it all up and slaps an "out of service" sign on it. He tried to like Delmar, but he couldn't.

"You need me more than you know," Delmar said.

"Maybe," Silas said. "Why's that?"

"Because I know something even Big Daddy up there don't know. Big hundred dollar man. Sheeit, what I know is worth ten times that."

"You don't know your ass from a Krispy Kreme, boy. You're just making stuff up so you can get paid like your old man. Well, you ain't me, and you don't get paid like me."

"You're not hearing me, is all I'm sayin'," Delmar said. "I'm sayin' I know something you don't."

"Then tell me," Silas said. "If it's worth anything to me, I'll pay you for it." He changed lanes and accelerated past the slower traffic. The quicker he could get to the church and run his bluff, the better. Not just to close the case, but to be done with these two. Danny had semblances of being tolerable, but Delmar was not. He was insufferable and he smelled bad. After only a few minutes of having him in the car, Silas was afraid his smell was going to completely consume the Oldsmobile and drive any remaining trace of his wife out of the car forever.

Delmar was quiet for several miles, which told Silas he had nothing new to tell. He wasn't disappointed, because he wasn't surprised. Delmar was a bullshitter who had been raised by a bullshitter. He could use them to move this case forward, though. The father and son wouldn't even need to get out of the car at the church. Silas had called Bob Parks and set up an appointment. His plan was to tell Bob that he was on his way to the State Police because Danny and Delmar had found another key piece of evidence which would cause the case to be re-opened, because what they found will without a doubt reveal the identity of the killer. He would tell Bob that he wanted to give him a heads up because it could potentially cause some trouble with the Will, and he didn't want him to be caught off guard, since he had been so helpful during the investigation. That last part was true. Unless, of course, Bob was involved in the murder. In that case, he had been the opposite of helpful. Either way, telling him this with Beverly close enough to overhear, should flush her out. It wasn't a perfect plan, because Beverly might just do nothing. But usually, guilty people, when they think they are about to be caught, either run, or they get really sloppy. At the very least, this stuck case might get unstuck.

At the church, Silas once again parked between the van and the little truck. "Wait here," he said, as he opened the car door and instinctively reached for his cigarettes.

"I saw that van at the quarry," Delmar said from the backseat. "A month before we found the wheelchair. I knew it was there, because I saw the woman who threw it in. That's what I know. How much is that worth?"

Silas leaned down quickly and stuck his head back in the car. "You did? No bullshit?"

"I did," Delmar said. He turned to his father. "You remember when your gout flared up 'cause you ate my share of the cornbread even though I was saving it? And I told you it was God punishing you because you always ate more than your share?"

"I remember," Danny said. He looked frustrated with the boy, but that seemed not uncommon.

"Yeah, so I had to go fishing alone," Delmar said. "And that night, this van pulled up, and I sat back in the dark, and watched. When she opened the sliding door, the inside light came on, and then when she unfolded the ramp, another light came on, like a floodlight almost, and it lit her up like high Noon."

"And you saw this lady clearly enough to identify her?" Silas asked.

"Does a bear sleep in the woods?" Delmar asked.

"I've never known a bear to sleep out in the woods," Danny said. "They like caves and dens and the like."

"The answer is yes," a frustrated Delmar said. "Now how much did I earn?"

"I'm torn," Silas said to Danny as he nodded towards Delmar. "I want to believe him, but I'm not sure I can. He could just point out the first woman I showed him."

"He could," Danny said. "You're not wrong."

"I won't," Delmar said. "But I don't have any way of convincing you other than just saying, I won't."

"I'm gonna trust you," Silas said. Because somehow, this redneck had become his best chance at solving this case. "I want both of you to stay here. "I'll come back and get you when I know she is in there. I'm gonna meet with the pastor real quick and try to see how much he knows. Try to read his face."

"Hell, I know what she looks like. Let's just bust up in there and I'll start finger gunning the damn room like I'm eenie meenie miney moeing the hell out of everyone in there, except I know who I'm gonna land on. That killer lady. Catch a killer by the toe. You damn right I will. The wheelchair murderess is what the crime podcasts will call her."

"What the hell do you know about podcasts?" Danny asked.

"I found an ipad at the Safeway a few months ago. And it had some crime podcasts saved on it. Hot Girls and Cold Cases is my favorite."

Silas interrupted. "Stay here." He stared at Delmar until he was convinced that the boy would stay in the car before he walked to the church and knocked on the side door.

Beverly answered the door and looked surprised. "May I help you?" she asked. She didn't seem happy to see him, but that might not mean anything, since she seemed to never be happy in general. Not a great look for a church secretary, in Silas' opinion.

"You remember me?" Silas asked. "I'm the private detective that was hired by Tucker Robertson's son to–"

"Of course," she said with a forced movement of her lips that she may have thought was a smile or most likely wanted everyone else to think it was.

"I'm here to see Bob," Silas said.

"Reverend Parks?" she corrected.

"That's the one," Silas said, as he sat down on the couch along the wall before she could walk him to the sanctuary to wait.

For a long moment, Silas could feel the woman staring at him. He had eventually gotten used to women settling their gaze on him over the years, but this wasn't a positive stare he was receiving. Part of him wanted to look up and force her to look away, but instead, he moved his eyes to his boots and waited for her to walk away. Finally, she did. The pastor's office was only a short distance away, down a short hall, and she moved their quickly, knocked, and entered the office. Muffled voices could be heard. If he tried hard, he could almost make out what they were saying. That was exactly what he wanted.

A minute passed, and then Pastor Bob came out of his office with Beverly right behind him. She didn't look worried or scared. She looked annoyed. "Next time, call, please," she said, as Bob waved to Silas.

When Silas stood up and passed Beverly on the way to Bob's office, he said, "You're not leaving are you ma'am?"

She gave him a confused look. "I'm here all day," she said, with an obvious edge to her voice.

"Good to know," Silas said, as he walked into Bob's office and closed the door behind him.

"Have a seat," Bob said, as he waved at two chairs in front of his desk. "Are you here to talk about the case more in depth?"

"I don't think that's gonna be necessary," Silas said. The State Police have been notified, and they have a few policemans on the way." It was the second lie he had told a church leader in less than a day.

"And why is that?" Bob asked.

"Because in a moment, I'm going to bring in a man who can identify the killer, and he's going to point out your secretary as the woman he saw bring Tucker Robertson to the quarry a few weeks before he was killed.

"What?" Bob said. He leaned forward and then backward, before leaning forward again.

Was he faking his surprise? It was hard to tell. Silas reminded himself to stay focused on the plan. If Bob was in on it, the truth would probably come out eventually. If Helen confessed, that was most important. Even if her motivation was to protect her church and her pastor, she would eventually implicate him if he was guilty. "I wanted to give you the respect of telling you face to face," Silas said. The first connection was the fact that she's driving Tucker Robertson's van."

"Well that part I can explain," Bob said. "The church inherited Tuck's estate, and my wife, who is the church administrator, got our board's approval to give the van to her as a gift. Her other car was always in the shop. She had nothing but trouble with it."

"Did the church give the van to her after Tucker died, or before?"

"It would have been after of course," Bob said. "I can ask my wife, she's here."

"Your wife works here with you?" Silas asked.

"No, she's a volunteer administrator," Bob said. "She stops in on her days off from her full time job." Bob pushed a button on the phone on his desk.

The phone made a beeping sound, and a woman's voice on the other end said, "Let me guess. You can't live without me."

Bob blushed. "I've got a question for you, honey. And I have a visitor here in my office. You're on speaker."

"Okay," the voice said. "What can I help you with?" She suddenly sounded business-like.

"Tucker Robertson's van," he said. "When did we give that to Beverly?"

"I don't know. A few weeks ago. After the will was read."

"She's only been driving it for a few weeks?" Bob asked.

"That's right," she said. "If that's all you need from me, I'm going to head on home."

Bob pushed a button on the phone and the speaker beeped off. He picked up the receiver. "Are you okay, Ellen? I thought you were working all day." He listened for a moment and then said, "Okay. Well, I hope you feel better." He put the receiver back on the phone and looked up at Silas. "She's only had the van for a few weeks. Doesn't that clear her?"

Silas felt his stomach sink. How many times was he going to follow the wrong lead in this case? "I just need a moment, Pastor," Silas said quietly. "I'm going to ask my witness to come in and see Beverly. If he clears her, I will of course apologize to both of you."

"And the police?" Bob said. "I thought you had the State Police on the way."

Silas stared at him for a moment, trying to figure out what he meant. "Oh," he said quickly, remembering the lie. "I will cancel them if it turns out that Beverly isn't who he saw." Silas realized that Delmar probably would identify Beverly, because he was a con artist, and even a positive identification from him wouldn't matter. He was most likely going to go with whoever Silas put in front of him. He had worried that would happen and now that worry was a reality.

"And we're not worried about apologies," Bob said. "Beverly doesn't even know what you were accusing her of, and I understand where you're coming from. Being misunderstood is something I've been my whole life, it feels like. Try telling people in this day and age about a God who loves them enough to punish them when they do wrong."

"Not a big market for it, huh?" Silas said. He was still trying to wrap his mind around how this case had gone so sideways, especially after he put his full mind to it.

"Nope," Bob said. "My Grandfather was a minister. He was what they called a circuit rider. Went between churches that shared him as their pastor. Five different churches. They all stayed open and took care of their people. Every church was packed on Sunday. And they paid my grandfather. Gave him a house to live in. He wasn't rich and didn't wanna be, but he had everything he needed. Times have changed. A year ago, we almost lost this building. Numbers were so far down. Attendance and giving. Ellen had to get a full time job. I was cleaning other churches at night. Other churches. Their pastor would leave, and I would pass him on the way in, carrying my vacuum cleaner. So, no. You don't owe me any apologies. Especially for trying to find out who killed the man who saved this church, really."

Silas didn't know what to say, so he just nodded and looked towards the door. After a moment, he finally spoke. "I'll just bring my…the witness…I'll just bring him in."

Silas walked down the hallway and across the office, trying not to look at Beverly. She was at her desk and seemed to be trying not to look at him, either. When he opened the door, Delmar was already coming in. He was breathing heavily, like he had been running.

"Delmar," Silas said quickly, wanting to get this over with. He was certain now that this guy was a con artist liar who was about to embarrass him. "Is this the lady you saw at the quarry?"

"No," Delmar said, between deep breaths of air. "That's not her."

Silas felt two emotions collide inside his heart. Disappointment and anger. He started to push Delmar back out of the door in hopes of somehow salvaging the scene they had already caused.

"It was her!" Delmar shouted. He was pointing towards the parking lot, but all Silas could see was Danny on the edge of the paved lot, pointing towards a cloud of dust coming from the gravel road.

"Who?" Silas asked, trying to cut through his confusion.

"That lady who just came out of the church," Delmar said. "She came out real fast and got in her car and flew the hell out of here. Daddy tried to stop her, but she was going too fast."

Silas turned back around to Beverly. "Who just left here?" he asked quickly.

When she didn't answer, but instead started shouting into the intercom, "Reverend? Reverend? I think we have a problem out here", Silas knew the woman was Bob's wife.

Silas ran to the car and pulled out his keys as he flung open the door and started the car. "Get in!" he yelled at Danny who was still pointing down the road.

"Are we still gonna get weenies?" Delmar shouted over the roar of the Oldsmobile engine as he piled into the front seat.

"Brother, if you just broke this case the way I think you just did, I'll buy you all the weenies you can eat!"

Danny jumped in the back seat, and Silas pushed the gas pedal to the floor. Behind him, someone was shouting for him to wait, but he didn't listen.

"What kind of car was she driving?" Silas yelled, as he navigated the curves and turns on the gravel road.

"It was one of those rectangle looking things," Danny said. "I hate those damn cars, or whatever they are."

"Rectangle doesn't help me," Silas said. Gravel turned to asphalt and the muscle car began to move even faster. "What color was it?"

"It was red," Delmar said. "I guess it was parked on the other side of the building because I never even saw it until that woman ran past us and then that red car came flying around the corner and down the road."

Where the side road met the highway up ahead, Silas knew he was going to have to make a choice. Right or left? His instincts said right, because that's the easiest and fastest turn to make, but he looked ahead quickly and after seeing faint tire tracks turning left, he jerked the wheel of the Oldsmobile and accelerated onto the highway just as a UPS truck barreled past, making Silas drop the car off the right shoulder of the road to avoid a collision. He corrected quickly and jammed the gas pedal to the floor.

"We almost diiiiied!" Delmar shouted as he slunk his body out of the front seat and into the back with his Daddy.

The car tires squealed as Silas made a fast turn around a narrow curve. He accelerated again when the road straightened and then tapped the brakes to make a left turn so sharp that Danny hit the side window. As soon as Silas straightened the car, he hit another curve, throwing Delmar against the glass this time.

Up ahead, Silas saw a car. Was it red? No. It was orange, and it was a Jeep. "That's not her is it?" he called out over his shoulder.

"No," Delmar said from the backseat. "I told you it was red. And rectangle!"

Silas crossed the yellow lines and sped up to pass the Jeep. As he did, a smaller car, one of those hybrids, slowly pulled out of a side road and into the lane Silas was using. He passed the Jeep and whipped back in front of the Jeep just in time for the hybrid to pass, going in the other direction. The hybrid beeped. It sounded like one of Pete's old squishee toys.

Just as Silas was thinking he had chosen the wrong direction, and Bob's wife must have turned right out of the church road, he spotted a red, oddly shaped vehicle ahead of him. "Is that her?" he shouted, as his right foot made the engine roar.

"Yayeppppp!" Delmar shouted as he climbed back into the front seat. "Winner Winner Weiner Dinner!"

Silas couldn't help but be amazed at how ludicrous this situation had become so quickly. The pastor's wife was the killer? And now they were chasing her in Silas' wife's car, with one redneck asshole riding shotgun, while the redneck asshole's redneck asshole father was in the back seat. What was her motive? It was an odd time to be asking that question, but as Silas was closing the gap between his car and hers, his mind found it an important enough question to push it to the forefront.

Her motive could be the exact same as Beverly's. She was protecting her church. Her motive could be even more intense than Beverly's. Bob had said the church was having trouble before Tucker died. If his wife was the church administrator, she would have felt those financial woes just as much as her husband. She may have even known more about the problems the church was having than Bob even did.

A tow truck pulled out of a side road and got behind Bob's wife. Whoever was driving it was in a hurry to get onto the highway, but once he had cut Silas off, he didn't seem in a hurry any longer. Silas pulled his foot off of the gas and moved the car to the left to try to see around the truck. The problem was, the tow truck was riding the center line already, so Silas had to keep whipping the Oldsmobile back to the right to avoid being hit by oncoming traffic as he checked for a break big enough to pass. Silas swerved to the right, checked, saw no gap, and swung back to the right. He did it again and saw a possible gap, but cursed himself for not taking it. At this point, the red car was almost out of view ahead, and the tow truck seemed to be slowing down.

"She's not in that truck," Delmar shouted from the passenger seat. He thumped the dashboard and yelled, "Speed up dammit! You've got to pass this asshole now!"

It may have been his anger at Delmar, or his determination not to let Bob's wife escape (or both) that made him shout like his favorite wrestler growing up as he jerked the wheel to the right, hit the gas, and passed the slow ass tow truck on the shoulder, all while yelling "Woooooooooooooo!" at the top of his lungs.

"That's how it's done!" Danny yelled from the back seat, breaking his silence finally. "That. Is. How. It. Is. Done, baby!" He kicked the back of Delmar's seat for emphasis between every word.

"Stop kicking her seat!" Silas yelled as he fought to close the gap between the Oldsmobile and the red car.

"I'm not a her!" Delmar shouted.

Silas actually considered explaining he meant his wife, since he still considered the Oldsmobile her car, but he decided against it and instead shouted another, "Wooooooooo!" for good measure.

Finally, he was within a few car lengths of Bob's wife. Bob had called her Ellen. He was finally catching up to Ellen when it occurred to him that he had no siren, and no official capacity within which he could pull her over. He didn't have a phone to call the police, and the CB in the Oldsmobile hadn't worked for years.

"Ram her!" Delmar yelled. "Ram that bi–"

"Shut up!" Silas yelled back. He needed to think, but Delmar yelling from the front seat and Danny cackling from the back seat because he found Silas yelling at his son entertaining, was making it impossible for Silas to even consider what he should do next, except make sure Ellen and her red Kia didn't get away. He wasn't sure he had ever seen a Kia Soul before, but when Delmar described it as rectangular, he wasn't wrong. In fact, the damn car was so ugly in Silas' mind that he began to be just as angry with the Soul as he was with Ellen, and she was possibly a cold blooded killer.

Once he got close enough to see Ellen look back at him through her rear view mirror, he realized she looked familiar. Had she been at the church when he was there before? No. Even with the obscured view he had of her, a recognition grabbed hold of him that he couldn't quite place. It was recent. Not at the church. While he was trying to figure out where he had seen Bob's wife before, a boy on a bike, barely ten years old, if that, pedaled down his driveway and towards the Kia Soul, which was trying to accelerate and leave Silas behind. Silas hit his horn so hard he thought he might press it into the steering wheel. At the same time, he left off the gas and pulled the Oldsmobile off of the road and let it coast to a stop. The boy on the bike had stopped well before reaching the road, but just seeing how that could have turned out in such a bad way caused Silas to come to his senses. He wasn't a cop anymore. He couldn't just decide to pursue some suspect in a big car chase. This wasn't the movies, or Magnum P.I.

"What the hell are you doing?" Delmar shouted. "She's gettin' away hoss!"

"We're gonna call the highway patrol," Silas said as he fumbled for his lighter.

"Yo your hands are shakin' like an oak tree," Delmar said.

"Trees don't shake," Danny said calmly. "And there's a big van behind us," Danny called out from the back seat. "I think he was followin' us."

"What?" Silas asked, caught off guard. "How? There's no way? Is it the pastor?"

"No, it's not a church van," Danny said. His voice was calm, and it suddenly occurred to Silas that being followed or chased was probably old hat for Danny and Delmar.

"Why didn't you say something, Daddy?" Delmar asked. "That's a dumbass move on your part. I'm just sayin'."

"I was more worried about that damn red car," Danny said to Silas while ignoring his son.. "And I was in shock that Delmar was telling the truth. And right about something. Neither one happens often, and never at the same time!"

Silas let the realization that he had been followed, probably even before he pulled into the church, settle into his mind. Thinking through it, he rejected several plans, most of which revolved around another car chase, and with the adrenaline still flowing through him from the chase that had just ended, he decided to step out of the car and find out what these guys wanted.

His fingers had barely touched the door handle before Silas was thrown into the steering wheel. He pushed himself back against his seat just in time to hear a crashing sound as he was thrown forward into the steering wheel again. This time, he felt heat on his forehead as blood trickled down onto his nose, and then dripped onto his jeans. Silas didn't remember opening the car door, but he suddenly felt himself swaying as he walked towards the van. The last thing he saw was three men with baseball bats emerge from a side door of the can.

Silas didn't feel the blow that sent him sprawling to the sidewalk, but he did stay conscious long enough to read the words on the van's driver side door. Vickerson Pawn and Loan.

Chapter 13

For the second time in just a few days, Silas woke up with Tommy and Jenny in the room. Just like before, he had a headache and he was disoriented. This time the headache was worse, but based on the monitor hooked to him and the type of bed he was in, he immediately knew where he was. He had been taken to the hospital. He wasn't sure how long he had been there, and he tried to ask Tommy or Jenny, but he couldn't make the words come. He heard Jenny tell Tommy to go alert a nurse that he was awake, but he must have fallen asleep again, because he woke up to a dimly lit room with no one in there but a nurse who was asking if he knew his name and date of birth. After forcing out the answers she wanted, he managed to ask her to call the State Police. "The local police are already here," she said. "I'm supposed to let them know as soon as you're conscious and feel up to talking."

"What time is it?" Silas asked. The pain in his head was gone, probably because of medication. He checked quickly to make sure he wasn't cuffed to the bed, and breathed a sigh of relief when he saw that he wasn't.

"It's about 8:30," the nurse said. "At night."

Silas tried to calculate how long it had been since he had lost consciousness. Six or seven hours. Maybe eight? He couldn't remember. "You can tell them to come in anytime," Silas said. He tried to straighten up in the bed and that's when he noticed his left arm and his right leg were both in casts. "Damn," he growled softly to himself.

Some time passed before two uniformed police officers walked into his room. One was a local police officer, but much to his relief, the other was a state policeman. "Mr. Buchanan?" the policeman asked.

"That's me," Silas said. "I'm awful glad to see you." Then he quickly added, "Both of you."

"I'm Patrolman Johnson, and this is Officer Wetzezky." After Johnson approached the bed, leaned over and shook Silas' hand, Wetzezky just nodded and raised a hand from near the door where she had remained standing since they walked in.

"We've got a few questions for you," Johnson said. "Quite a few, as you can imagine."

"I'll answer every one," Silas said. "But there's a murderer on the loose. Murderess? Alleged. If I can tell you about her, that will help you all not lose any more time. She's probably in another state by now, but the trail isn't cold yet."

"She's already in our custody," Wetzezky said.

"She is?" Silas asked. "How?" He felt a wave of nausea hit him and he had to close his eyes for a minute.

"Her husband brought her in," Johnson said. "You okay?" he asked Silas.

After Silas nodded, the Patrolman continued. "He walked right in the station with her, about the same time you were being admitted here."

"She confessed to all of it," Wetzezky added.

"Why did she do it?" Silas asked. "Please tell me it was about more than just money. Was there an affair or something? Anything?"

"No," Wetzezky snapped. "She was trying to save the church. And her husband."

Silas noticed her tone change. Like she was defending the woman who had confessed to drowning a paralyzed man.

"Now the church is fine and he's fine and dandy, but she's sitting in the same jail she works at," she continued. "It's not right."

"Huh?" Silas said quickly. "She worked at the jail?"

"She was a civilian employee for their department," Johnson said, as if he were trying to explain why Officer Wetzezky was so obsessed.

Civil Servant Ellen. She was Bob's wife. The woman who killed Tucker Robertson. He tried to wrap his aching head around this. "So it's over?" Silas asked. It was more like he was saying it to himself than asking either of the cops. "Just like that?"

"Oh it's not over," Johnson said. "There's still a lot of questions we have for you. And you're probably going to lose your investigator's license. Or have it suspended at least. Driving like you did."

"How are the guys who were in the car with me? Are they okay?" Silas asked.

"Not a scratch on either of them," Johnson said. "The father ran them off with what we now know was your pistol."

"You're not particular about who you ride around with, are you?" Wetzezky said.

"About as particular as you are about who you worked with," Silas said.

Johnson raised his hand up. "Come on now. They are actually the ones who helped break the case," he said to Wetzezky. Then he turned to Silas. "They called my barracks while you were being transported here. Told us enough of the story to bring us in on this, alongside the local Police. At that point no one knew the conflict of interest, but they knew enough to call us in." He looked back at Wetzezky. "Based on the locals ruling this one a suicide early on, I suppose."

"So what's next?" Silas asked.

"Like I said, we had some questions. Most of them can wait until you're out of here in a few days. You can come by the barracks station and meet with me for a bit. For now, we just need to know what you know about the guys in the van. Any idea who they were?"

"The van was from Vickerson Pawn and Loan. I had a run in with them earlier this week. They kidnapped the man who hired me, and shot my dog."

Wetzezky made a sound and shook her head. Silas turned and looked at her, but decided to choose his battles.

"Damn," Johnson said. "What kind of asshole kills a man's dog? I hope you made them pay for it."

Silas didn't respond to that. Instead, he asked. "Do I need to swear out a formal complaint against them? For my dog, and for what happened today?"

Johnson looked at him for a moment, and then turned to Wetzezky. "Officer, do you mind giving us a moment?"

"Why?" she asked. "I think we'd better question him together."

"I've got jurisdiction," Johnson said sharply. "That's why."

Wetzezky made a face like she had just tasted something spicy, then turned and left the room. It looked like she tried to slam the door, but the hinges were set for a slow close, so it didn't work out for her.

After Wetzezky was gone, Johnson turned to Silas. "I would let this go. This thing with the guys in the van. Unless you think they had something to do with the murder."

"I don't think so," Silas said. "I think they were trying to defend their pastor."

"The suspect's husband?" Johnson asked.

"No," Silas said. Suddenly he felt very tired. "It's a long damn story. I don't think they're a danger to anyone but me, so when I come by the barracks I will tell you about them too."

"I will ask Ms. Parks if they had anything to do with it," Johnson said. "At this point, she seems to be cooperating."

"So that's that," Silas said. "I've done law work long enough to know that not every case ends with fireworks, but this one…I guess I've done everything I need to do."

"Come on by the barracks, like I said. I just need a few things for my report. But, yeah, she confessed, so there isn't anything else left for you to do."

"What happens with the will?" Silas asked. "Does everything go to his son, now?"

"Oh I don't know," Johnson said. "I suppose it does. Maybe. It sure won't go to Wren River. An administrator with the beneficiary can't kill someone and still expect to inherit his estate. Surely, not."

"Surely not," Silas said as he felt his head slowly numb. He tried to say goodbye to the state policeman, but couldn't stay awake long enough. He fell asleep to all the other surely nots in his mind. Would he make any money off of this case? Surely not. Would he have ever guessed that Civil Servant Ellen was Ellen the pastor's wife, and Ellen the cold blooded killer? Surely not.

Chapter 14

Silas heard Tommy plowing snow before he could even see his headlights. Snow was either falling too hard to see the truck, or it was on the other side of one of the trailers and out of sight. Tommy was supposed to wake Silas up once the snow started, but he didn't. Most likely, he wanted to show what he could do on his own now that he was completely in charge of maintaining the grounds of the trailer park. In exchange for landscaping, moving snow, and general maintenance, he lived there for free. This gave Silas more time for his investigation business, which had picked up quite a bit over the last several months.

Over by the front of the lots, was Danny, whose cursing could be heard over the sound of the snowblower he was operating. Danny lived in the trailer by the dumpsters. Silas had made an agreement with him where he would pay rent when he could, or he would trade work when he couldn't. Also, he was allowed to pull anything he wanted from the dumpsters, in exchange for being available to crawl, dive, or slither somewhere Silas didn't want to go, in order to retrieve evidence for whatever case Silas happened to be working on at the time. Many a time, Danny had paid rent by selling what he had pulled out of the dumpster or fished out of the quarry. Delmar wasn't currently living with him, as he was serving the back end of an eight month jail sentence for selling copious amounts of aluminum and copper he had stolen from a trailer park. That park just happened to be the one owned by Silas, and the trailer he had partially dismantled belonged to Jenny, who shot him twice with a 410 shotgun she usually used to threaten customers. Delmar claimed she was trying to kill him, but she had aimed for his ass and had managed to hit both cheeks.

The Tucker Robertson case was in his rear view mirror except for one item of business he would conclude before lunchtime. He hadn't even thought about the case for a long while until back in September when he had seen the story about Bodean Culp forming his church into an international corporation, along with an online college. The man on the evening news interviewed the new CFO who would be in charge of the millions of dollars this venture expected to bring in over the next few years. That project was seeded by the sale of Robertson Quarry stock, which the church had inherited. The story had surprised Silas at first. He was shocked when he heard the CFO's voice and then read the name printed under the familiar face. After a bit, it had angered him. Finally, though, after Silas had decided what he would do about it, he felt pretty good about the whole deal which would be, for him at least, a closed case by the end of the day.

First, he needed to swing by the back of the park and pick up his new business partner who, since October, had taken over the management of both the trailer park and the detective agency. This freed

Silas up even more to do what he did best-solve cases. Sometimes his new partner would help him with cases, too, and he had gotten quite good at it. For what Silas needed to do today, he figured it would help if he had someone with him to keep things calm.

As he pulled his truck up in front of Bob Parks' trailer, the former pastor of Wren River Baptist Church came out in a big coat and one of those Russian style hats. When he opened the truck door, Silas was already laughing at him.

"What?" Bob asked defensively. "It's ten degrees out, and snowing. I don't wanna catch a cold."

"You're not gonna catch anything with that getup," Silas said, still laughing. "But I don't need you to catch anybody on this run. I just need you to keep me from killing him."

Bob was good at keeping Silas on track and calm. In sticky situations, he was the cooler head that usually prevailed. In addition to that and handling the money end of things, Bob also acted as an ambassador between Silas and the local Police. Most of them still liked Bob, and blamed Silas for the arrest of Ellen, who most of them also still liked. At first, Silas assumed they had ruled Tucker Robertson's death a suicide in order to protect Ellen, but it ended up being as simple as the lead investigator wanting to quickly wrap up a case involving the richest man in town's son. Deeming it a suicide would mean far less paperwork. At least until Silas Buchanan poked his nose into it. That's how most of the local police saw it. He couldn't leave well enough alone. A con man was dead. Who cared how it happened? In their minds, Ellen Parks should still be Ellen the Civil Servant, instead of Ellen the inmate. In their minds, Ellen was one of the victims. And so, too was her husband Bob. The police liked Bob. They did not like Silas. Silas didn't mind that too much, since he now had Bob to talk to the police on his behalf, on any occasion such became necessary.

As Silas had originally suspected, once Tucker Robertson's death was found to be a homicide, and the person convicted of the crime was the administrator of the church who inherited the estate of the murdered man, the will was ruled void and negated. The man who was on the previous last will and testament of Tucker Robertson immediately filed a civil suit to have the original will honored, since the new will had been ruled void. Bodean Culp's case was all but made when Ellen Parks testified that her sole motive for murdering Tucker Robertson was because Wren River Baptist was having financial problems and Tucker's death meant they would never have to worry about money ever again.

As they neared Abba's House, Silas rolled his window down a crack and pulled out his pack of cigarettes. As he shook one out, Bob noticed and shook his head. "I thought you were cutting back," he said.

"I have. I only smoke in stressful situations now," Silas said.

"Your whole life is a stressful situation."

"Not now that you're taking care of all the stuff I hate doing," Silas responded.

"Why are you stressed out now?" Bob asked.

"I'm worried."

"Worried about what?"

"Worried that I will pound that skinny little bastard into the concrete," Silas said, as he lit the cigarette.

"Well, I'm here to make sure you don't."

"You should want to lay a beating on him worse than I do."

"Why?"

"Because he caused your wife to end up in jail. You lost your church. Hell, you lost everything because of this spoiled little–"

"He didn't cause Ellen to kill Tuck," Bob said. "Ellen caused Ellen to kill that man. And trust me, I've blamed myself for many months now, but I had to stop. For my own insanity, I had to stop. I can't let myself off the hook, and still blame this guy."

"He's a damn con man, and he is working for a con man. And you can't blame him?"

"I can blame him for being a con man, yes. I said I couldn't blame him for Tuck's murder, or for me losing the church."

"Well, you can kind of blame him for you losing the church," Silas said as he passed a massive sign showing the expansion plan for what was now being called Abba's House International, Incorporated. "I mean look at that. If he hadn't opened the investigation back up, and using me to solve the case, you could be building this big...whatever it is."

"It's a monstrosity," Bob said. Anyone that thinks building something like that would make Jesus happy, has read a different Testament than the New Testament. I can tell you that much. Why are you turning in here? I thought we were going to the church offices across town to serve the papers there."

"Well," Silas said, as he tossed his smoked down cigarette out through the cracked window before rolling it up tightly. "I did some investigatin'. You know I do a bit of that on the side."

"I've heard rumors," Bob said.

"Me too," Silas said with a smile. "So I did some of that investigatin' that I'm rumored to do from time to time, and I found out that Abba's House International, Incorporated is having their New Year's Eve party at the old Ambassador Hotel, which they purchased earlier this year and remodeled. Since all of them will be in one place, I thought there was no better opportunity to serve them notice than right there, especially since they're all gonna probably be snowed in together for a few days. It will give them lots of time to read through all these court documents, and then answer all the questions they're asked to the fullest satisfaction of everyone who's asking." Silas slowed the truck to a crawl and used his turn signal to let the long line of traffic behind him know that he was turning left into the hotel parking lot, which was already filled with cars.

Silas looked over at Bob as he opened the door and stepped out into four inches of snow. Bob extended his hand and made a motion that Silas understood. He responded by taking the revolver from his shoulder holster and handing it to Bob, who promptly locked it in the glove compartment before stepping out of the passenger side of the truck and walking towards the hotel.

The wind blew the still falling snow in a swirl and for a moment, Silas lost sight of Bob. "Don't forget your briefcase. We need that," Silas said.

"Got it," Bob said, as he lifted the case to show him. "Now remember. You have to serve a set of the papers to Bodean and the same set to Larry. As the newly named CFO of Abba's House International, we made sure he was named on every lawsuit as a co-conspirator."

"How many plaintiff's did it total up to?" Silas asked.

"Two hundred and forty-seven," Bob said.

"And Larry can be named as a defendant, even though he wasn't around when Culp and his daddy cheated all those churches and people?"

"He won't end up being found liable," Bob said. "But it sure will make for a bad year for young Larry Robertson."

"Oh yeah," Silas said quickly as he swung open the main door of the hotel, letting music and laughter and cheering spill out into the cold. "Did you include in that stack of papers, my bill of services that he never paid?"

"I sure did," Bob said. "And I charged him interest."

"I like this vengeful side of you Bob," Silas said.

"I'm not vengeful. But I've turned so many cheeks, I don't have any more left to turn. I used to just let people run right over me, but Jesus didn't intend for us to be a doormat."

"Well, you're definitely not that way anymore, Bob," Silas said. "You've helped convince almost two hundred and fifty churches to sue Bodean Culp into oblivion for almost two decades of fraud and conspiracy. That's not the work of a doormat."

"Bob the doormat was the old me," he said. "And the old man is dead."

The End

Jason Queen grew up in the Blue Ridge Mountains of Virginia where he is now raising his five children with his wife, Misty. His lifelong dream of writing and publishing a novel was fulfilled with *My Life Was Mercy Creek* and he recently published the sequel, *The World Comes To Mercy Creek.*

Jason works as a paralegal in a law firm, and he is a part owner and book brewer with The Independent Literature Brewing Company, an independent imprint based in Winchester, Virginia. When he isn't working or writing, Jason loves to canoe and fish with his family and read novels of all different genres, but his favorites are historical fiction and westerns. The recurring themes a reader can usually find in Jason's writings include nostalgic references and traditions, individuals or families overcoming adversity, and the exploration of the American Dream.

Check out these other titles from Indie Lit!

My Life Was Mercy Creek is a coming of age story told from the point of view of a boy growing up in Virginia during the Great Depression. Will the Morrissey family rise together from the depths or scarcity or will the brutal realities of the rural world they live in separate them and destroy their hopes and dreams?

The World Comes To Mercy Creek is a continuation of the series of Morrissey Family Novels. The year is 1941, and threats of War from across the ocean combined with bulldozers, bank robbers, and a mystery on the moun-tain to jeopardize not only the families of this rural Virginia community, but a way of life that values the pursuit of life, liberty, and happiness above progress, power, and politics.

At Indie Lit we love summertime and we love short stories, so we decided to combine those ingredients and create our own *Summer Brew*. This collection of stories was written by six authors of varied backgrounds, styles, and experience. There's a little something for everyone in this collection, and we hope you enjoy each and every one of them!

Don't Miss

Come Home To Mercy Creek

by Jason L. Queen

The third and final installment of The Morrissey Family Novels trilogy will be available to read by the end of 2021. World War 2 comes to an end and brings with it a homecoming for some and heartbreak for others.

Coming soon to

WWW.BOOKBREWERS.COM

Other Dirt Road Crime Stories

You never know where a dirt road will lead...

We took the crime novels our dads used to enjoy in their recliners (and some moms read after we went to bed) and southern fried them.

Find more dirt road crime at

www.BOOKBREWERS.COM

Made in the USA
Middletown, DE
04 March 2022

61997427R00094